The
Childkeeper

The Childkeeper

SOL STEIN

HARCOURT BRACE JOVANOVICH

New York and London

Library of Congress Cataloging in Publication Data

Stein, Sol.
The Childkeeper.
I. Title.
PZ4.S8195Ch   [PS3569.T375]   813'.5'4   75-15823
ISBN 0-15-117233-1

B C D E

To Robin

who taught me

what natural meant

ACKNOWLEDGMENTS

Editing an editor is like operating on a surgeon who is fully awake and watching every move critically. And so two of my friends, Tony Godwin and Patricia Day, deserve citations for bravery as well as my gratitude for seeing me through the several drafts of this book

I am also indebted to Michaela Hamilton for her astonishing first reaction and her subsequent instant replays that were so helpful; to my friend Judge Charles L. Brieant, Jr. for his supralegal brief; and to Edward G. DiLoreto for his advice on police procedures.

The characters and situations in this work
are wholly fictional and imaginary, and
do not portray and are not intended to portray
any actual persons or parties.
—Franz Kafka, *The Trial*

Parents begin by loving
their children; as they
grow older they judge them;
sometimes they forgive them.*

* With apologies to Oscar Wilde

1

ROGER MAXWELL was a man whose time had come. He had learned to enjoy his wife. He began to reconcile himself to the fact that his four children were at times lovable and at other times mischievous. He sent a tax-deductible tithe—but not himself—to church. He tolerated his government. When faced with younger men who were bearded, he felt unfashionable. Yet Roger Maxwell was secure. He reserved himself not for transient lovers or friends, but for himself and Regina, a couple, even by Noah's standards, deserving of safe passage.

One day recently, at the bank where he had been employed for more than a quarter of a century, as he was putting some papers into his briefcase to read on the commuter train, he was suddenly summoned into the Directors' room, where, amidst champagne and congratulations, it was revealed that he had attained a senior vice presidency, the highest rank available to a man totally unrelated by blood to the family that had for six generations supplied the bank with its chief executive officers. If on Roger Maxwell's way home that day the devil had tapped him on his shoulder and inquired about his remaining ambitions, he would have said only "to live."

With his promotion and its attendant raise, Roger could now afford to shuck his no longer suitable house and find his ideal somewhat farther from the city. And so he inquired about for the name of the best real estate agent in the vicinity of Chappaqua and Pleasantville. His friends suggested Stickney's.

"Children?" asked Stickney.

"Four," said Roger. "One's away at college, but we've got to keep a room for him."

"Guests?"

"Sometimes. Especially the children. They like to have their friends sleep over."

"Any preference in styles?"

Roger wanted to say a solid-brick federal, but he knew Regina didn't agree, and so he said just, "An older house, with some distinction, and at least two or three acres of ground."

Stickney, who had been flipping through his cards, said, "There're five right now. Could you come up Sunday, say at two?"

"Of course."

"You'll bring the children?"

"Yes."

Stickney was pleased. Children were part of his strategy.

The Maxwells' Chrysler station wagon was taken to the car wash that auspicious Sunday in spring by Jeb, who at sixteen had recently acquired his junior license. And it was Jeb who was allowed to drive the Maxwells to Stickney's office, to give him, Mr. Maxwell thought, not only practice but a sense of pride. The oldest Maxwell child, Harry, was no longer a child, but a second-year student at Tufts. And so there were five Maxwells who embarked on the Sunday inspection tour, full of hope. Jeb, at the wheel, his parents slightly squeezed in the front seat beside him, and in the back, Theodore, twelve and called Dorry, and the only girl, Nancy, aged nine. For Roger Maxwell, putting away the snow tires, as he had just done, was as sure a sign of the earth's renewal as the pink and red and white azaleas in bud and bloom that could be seen almost everywhere in Tarrytown. He was glad they could now afford the roomier house that he and Regina longed for. He put his elbow out so that she could slip her arm through his. He could not have been happier.

Roger glanced to his left. Jeb had his eyes on the road. Good. He remembered how nervous he had been at sixteen when he himself had first started driving. Jeb seemed relaxed, his left elbow resting on the window, his right hand holding the wheel lightly, as if he had been driving all his life. Roger felt safe in Jeb's hands.

Dorry and Nancy were chattering away in the back. Dorry was anxious only that they should find a house in a community where he could continue his Little League playing, and hoped that now his father had been appointed Senior Vice President at the home office of the bank, they would at last stay put in a house that his mother found suitable to their circumstances.

The youngest Maxwell child, Nancy, was gleeful about house-hunting for a special reason. At nine she had already developed a business flair. She could bake her own cookies, which were much tastier than the commercial ones the Girl Scouts offered from door to door once each year. Nancy would put hers up by the dozen in cellophane lunch bags and take them around from house to house, offering them for sale, usually to neighbors or people who knew her family and would be too embarrassed not to buy something, though in some places Nancy had worn out her welcome. If a purchaser of her cookies subsequently met her in the street and said how good they were, Nancy would be at that neighbor's doorstep two or three times a month, package in hand. She, more than any member of the family, was elated by the opportunity presented by moving the family residence, which would open up a whole new field of prospects. And she was quite certain she could persuade her father to drive her to their old neighborhood every once in a while so she could surprise her old customers with continued service.

It had been twenty-four years since Regina Maxwell had left her parents' house in South Carolina. In her memory it had gradually become the pillared mansion she had wanted it to be, of a dimension still to be achieved in a house she shared with Roger and the children. The high excitement of the children affected her. She glanced around at them, remembering how as babies they proved to be inept compared to puppies and kittens who could run about and look after themselves soon after birth. Regina recalled the desperate coaxing, getting Harry to stand-without immediately plopping down, and no sooner was Harry running about the house on his own— though you needed eyes in back of your head to watch his constant falling in the direction of the sharp corners of low tables—the cycle started over again with Jeb, and then Dorry, and at last the last, Nancy.

Yet Nancy was growing so fast, Regina knew that soon her motherhood would be over, all her children would be grown, and she hated hated hated it coming to an end because it foredoomed her life. Despite all the measles, mumps, chicken pox that seemed like token deaths at the time each child lived through the crisis of fever and imagined dangers that the idiot pediatrician insisted on calling *normal childhood diseases,* it had turned out all right. They were handsome children, their bodies well formed, bright and eager and not horrid the way other children sometimes behaved. She felt wholly justified in her belief that the Almighty took a special interest in the genealogy of certain families. When she compared her children to those of some of her friends, it was as if the defects of the human race had been stayed from her brood, and she credited it to a blending of Roger's genes with her father's and her father's ancestors', who in legend at least were brave and gallant and rich. Regina felt personally blessed to have had Harry and Jeb and Dorry and Nancy conceived in her body, and to have brought them along to this moment, healthy and free of bodily imperfections.

She was lost in these thoughts as the station wagon left the parkway and wended its way along an unfamiliar country road. Suddenly Nancy squealed, "Hey, look, horses!"

There were indeed four horses behind a fence, and Jeb cut his eyes to the right for a split second and let the right wheels spin onto the shoulder, which threw up a spray of gravel and sent everyone's pulse spurting. Jeb instantly got the wagon back onto the asphalt, saying, "Sorry."

Neither adult said a word, for which Jeb was grateful. For the rest of the drive he kept both hands on the wheel.

The Chrysler finally pulled up in front of Stickney's. Mrs. Maxwell moved to the back seat with the younger children, and Jeb, his muscles aching from the tenseness of this first long drive with the family, stretched out in the back of the wagon as his father got behind the wheel and Mr. Stickney got in beside him to point the way.

Ralph Stickney's plan was to show the most unsuitable house first. And so he directed them to the Parker residence, which, predictably, disappointed them all with its ordinariness.

Regina Maxwell, who yearned for familiar landscapes still, felt her heart fibrillate when they drove up to the second house, an imitation colonial on the outskirts of Pleasantville;

it had an imposing circular drive leading up to four white pillars. She thought she saw two magnolias, though there were none on the property, and when she looked at the house a second time, she imagined the voices of darkies that had been the counterpoint of her childhood, a sound in her head that brought her tranquillity whenever Jeb and his friends turned their stereos high. But as her husband pointed out tactfully, for he would never consciously do anything to dislodge his wife's recollections of her idyllic childhood, the colonial had thirty-two rooms, and how would it be kept in order, this being 1973 and trustworthy servants hard to find and difficult to keep?

Maxwell lit up when he saw the third house, a federal with thick brick walls. Outside it seemed a fortress, but within, on close examination, the telltale signs of water damage were clear evidence of a roof in need of drastic repairs or replacement; he knew from experience that responsible roofers shunned new customers and that the unreliable others would have to be brought back again and again under duress to fix their own incompetent work. He could not knowingly let himself in for such headaches at a time when he was just settling into a position at the bank it had taken him years of politicking and good work to secure, and heading a department that needed drastic reorganization because of the incompetence of his predecessor.

Every Maxwell in the car knew at once that the fourth house, a sprawling clapboard dwelling in five wooded acres, just did not look like an abode suitable for a Senior Vice President of an important bank. It was roomy enough, and the isolation from other houses was in this day of encroachment an asset, but the clapboard exterior spoke of working-class taste. Inside, the rooms were boxy. Ralph Stickney cut the inspection short and hurried them to the Simeon King house.

•

Legend had it that when Simeon King, whose business was railroads and whose joy was hunting big game in the north woods, examined the architect's plans, he ordered the ceiling of the third story removed. He wanted to simulate a hunting lodge inside the house in a two-story space clear to the peaked roof of the attic to accommodate not only bunk beds but also the preserved carcasses of a female brown bear, a ten-point deer, a moose, and some smaller animals, including a mountain wildcat that he had shot. The taxidermist had excelled himself in immortalizing them because, like all merchants and artisans who dealt with Simeon King in the early years of the century, he dreaded the man's displeasure.

One day in 1933, Simeon King, said to be seventy-eight at the time, was sitting in a wing chair in his living room, reading the morning newspaper he loathed because it failed to print the news he willed to see in it, when a sudden severe pain in his head heralded a stroke. He was removed by volunteer ambulance to Brigham Memorial Hospital, the operating room of which had been built with funds donated entirely by Simeon at a time when the tax advantages of such beneficence were minuscule, and the gift had been received by the trustees as a genuine good deed.

The operating room was of no use in Simeon's case. The senior neurologist at Brigham solicited the advice of the man he had studied under, who gladly came when he heard the victim was Simeon King, and together they examined both the patient and the test results and came to the concerted conclusion that the stroke had been massive, disabling, and irreversible.

Simeon King, who had stalked large animals as if he were their master, now had an uncontrollable body, capable of only an occasional involuntary shudder. His mind, which had been characterized as incisive at Groton and Yale and subsequently by his competitors, could not cause his tongue to form words. His eyes communicated with the imprecision of an infant. He was incontinent as to both urine and bowels. Despite round-the-clock nursing care, the odor about him was pervasive; it offended Simeon's descendants, who came for a brief visit and did not return; it offended his wife, who remembered her love for him only when she was out of his presence and could recollect better times. Even the young doctor in residence, who had been instructed by the hospital's management to pay special attention to the patient in Suite A, found Simeon disgusting. He could have kept him alive for some weeks longer, but found no encouragement among members of the King family, who were solicitous about the inconvenience, and inquired casually about the likely cost. The young doctor sensed the inevitable. He was also weary from attending patients who could be helped. It is not known whether by commission or omission he snuffed the flicker of Simeon King's soul.

Simeon's assembled relatives, anxious to resolve the estate, now openly expressed their distaste for the hunting of animals, and urged the attorneys to dispose of the house that lodged them. His widow did not choose to oppose them, and began inquiries about living conditions in Palm Beach, where house servants might obey her instructions despite Simeon's absence.

Stickney's, the real estate agency used by knowledgeable families in that part of Westchester, took on the white elephant only because its geographic location fell within what the elder Stickney considered to be his exclusive territory. The market for big houses was slack in the trough of the Depression, and Stickney was embarrassed whenever he had to open the door to the upstairs room and explain that the widow King had promised to get rid of the stuffed animals when she moved after the house was sold.

In fact, the man who eventually bought the house was a

wealthy stockbroker named Sudliffe, who had sold short in 1928 and 1929. Sudliffe kept the animals on so that when he took clients or friends on a tour of the premises he'd have an excuse for mentioning that Simeon King himself had shot the beasts. Once the stockbroker's children were all bartered away to college or marriage, Sudliffe and his wife moved to a smaller house. The truth is that Sudliffe had never felt the house to be his. Everyone referred to it as the Simeon King house, and Sudliffe was delighted that his wife found a place built just two years previously by some executive whose company had shifted him elsewhere.

The Simeon King house changed owners several times during the next four decades, the Wentworths, the Hamiltons, the Searles, but all of its successive inhabitants resented living in a house that persisted in being known by the name of its original owner. When they moved away, it was presumably to find a home of their own. The Stickneys, father, son, and now grandson Ralph Stickney, didn't mind; they collected a commission each time the house changed hands.

What a striking contrast the huge Tudor was to the house the Maxwells had just seen. Its magnificent proportions were outlined against silver maples in full leaf. The bluestoned driveway, crunching under the tires, itself portended luxury no asphalt roadway could convey. The door to the house was massive, as if to provide room for giants to enter. And once inside, the entrance hall, with its polished marble floor, seemed too fine to walk on, though straight ahead the curving grand staircase beckoned them forward.

"The rooms are a good size," said Mr. Stickney, "but there are only thirteen of them as against thirty-two in the colonial. Let's look at the rooms on this floor first."

Regina's eyes took in the oblong living room, paneled in mahogany up to the height of a tall man, then white plaster for another six feet, a thin gold stripe at the top of each wall just a hair away from a similar gold stripe around the perimeter of the ceiling, with satyrs and nymphets, the kind she and Roger had seen in only the best hotels in Europe, chasing each other in relief around the border.

Nancy had curled herself into a sitting position inside the fireplace to demonstrate how huge it seemed to her, till a barely discernible shake of Mrs. Maxwell's head got her instantly out of there, thereby affirming Nancy's view of the unfairness of the strictures imposed by parental obedience.

"This must be a very expensive place," whispered Regina to Roger.

Her knowledgeable husband replied, "To build, not to buy. White elephants are negotiable."

Ralph Stickney's father had considered it his duty to present houses rather than to sell them. But Ralph had adjusted to the changed times. His responsibility was to himself. To make himself rich, he needed to be efficient in pushing a deal to conclusion. Two of the tactics he developed toward that end were to seem to knock some aspect of the house he proposed to sell and to side with the prospective purchaser against the absent seller.

"The kitchen has its drawbacks," he said to Mrs. Maxwell, leading them through the large dining room, which seemed an elongated version of the room they had just seen, through swinging double doors into a room walled with coppertone cabinets, with three or four gaps that made the room look like a mouth with missing teeth.

"They took the stove and built-in appliances with them," he said. "I told them it was a mistake."

Regina made a mental note to determine what the cost would be of replacement equipment and to ask Roger to bargain for that amount to be deducted from the finally agreed on price, should they decide on this place. She was of two minds:

what she had seen so far—the outside as you drove up to it, and the public rooms downstairs—would make visitors think Roger was the President of the bank instead of one of its numerous vice presidents; at the same time, it seemed so formal for a houseful of children who were never without friends and friends of friends, leaving untidiness in their wake. As she took a last look at the kitchen, she amused herself with the thought that it just didn't look like a place you'd dare make a peanut butter sandwich in.

"Well, shall we?" asked Mr. Stickney, escorting them through the entrance hall and to the foot of the main staircase leading to the bedrooms on the second floor.

He let the Maxwell children lead the way. The whole family, once they started inspecting, seemed suddenly activated, scurrying like mice in a picnic basket. For the Maxwells, each door-opening was a room-revelation, showing how much proportion and decoration could do to exude a sense of good taste and a richness that, for Roger Maxwell, soared beyond share-trading or the momentary value of the dollar abroad; it all seemed so permanent.

He took Regina to one side. "You could die in a house like this."

"What do you mean?"

"We'd never need or want a bigger one."

"Oh, I agree,'" she said. "It is . . ." She paused. If she said sumptuous or elegant he might misunderstand.

He helped her. "You're liking it."

"Do you think it's pretentious?"

"If it were a castle, you'd look perfectly at home."

Her father had flattered her like that all the years of her growing up. When she'd moved north to college, she'd found the men full of clever banter, but she missed the comforting rain of compliments until she met Roger. His first words to her had been *you are beautiful*. He hadn't even known her name.

Ralph Stickney let them have their moment together. He thought: The last flight will tell.

The staircase leading upward from the second floor was ordinary, a means of access, nothing more. The children had already started up.

"One moment," said Mr. Stickney on the stairs. He beckoned to Mr. and Mrs. Maxwell. When he had assembled them all on the third floor, he opened the door to the two-story-high forest of animals. Ralph Stickney thought of that room as the biggest, most elaborate playroom for children he had ever seen. He let Jeb and Dorry and Nancy enter first.

Nancy squealed when she saw the animals. Jeb went around stroking them as if they were alive. Dorry was in ecstasy, imagining the jealousy of the boys from his present neighborhood when they came to visit his new home.

Mr. Stickney invited the senior Maxwells to join him in the living room, where they could rest on the window seats, and he could, according to plan, go over with them the good and bad points of the various houses they had seen and draw up a balance sheet for contemplation.

"It's so much bigger than our present house," said Roger. "Our furniture will look lost."

"Oh, Roger," said Regina, "we have so much clutter now. The space is marvelous."

Maxwell glanced at the twelve-foot ceiling. He imagined their bulky housekeeper, Louise, up on a ladder dusting. They'd have to bring in a cleaning service. Extra expense.

"Now," said Mr. Stickney, "let's just make a list of the pros and cons. Then we can inspect the garden and the grounds." He had hardly begun to jot things down on his yellow pad when the children descended from their own private talk in the upstairs room and reason was flung to the winds as their unrelenting salesmanship was thrust at their parents. It had to be this house because of that room.

Mr. Stickney knew that though the children were the key to his strategy, he must never seem to side with them. "You've seen the five best houses I have right now," he said. "But if you'll be patient," he assured the Maxwells, "other large houses might come onto the market."

The three children looked at Ralph Stickney as if they wished him dead.

In the days that followed, each evening Jeb and Dorry and Nancy gave Roger and Regina no peace about their preference for the Simeon King Tudor. Roger was in no hurry to make a decision; he thought time was on his side. He suggested that their fourth and oldest offspring, no longer a child, should be summoned for his opinion.

A second visit to the house was arranged for a time when Harry could drive down from Tufts in his secondhand Austin and meet them there. Jeb led him immediately to the upstairs room with the bunk beds and stuffed animals. Harry sighed, thinking how his adolescent years might have been different had he been able to put his friends up overnight in a room like that.

That evening at dinner, the family, assembled for the first time in months, was invited by Roger to discuss the matter of the Simeon King house objectively.

When he said the word "objectively," he saw in the faces of the three youngest children the impossibility of reason in the real world. Only Harry, who now smoked a pipe as if he had been doing so all his life, was able to maintain a pose of studied calm.

Regina expressed a reservation about the mahogany-paneled dining room. She delighted in its elegant chandelier, which might fetch thousands in the marketplace if one was ever in a financial bind, though it would be barbaric to consider removing it from its setting. However, she feared that the formality of the room would require her to have the housekeeper serve dinner when they had guests; Regina had always preferred to do the serving herself, as her mother had done even when servants were ample. But hers seemed such a trivial reservation compared to the children's enthusiasm for the room with animals. Regina's sense of democracy required that if the children outnumbered her, their strong wishes should be acknowledged. Besides, she was completely taken by the spaciousness of it all, the high ceilings, the stairway that made just going upstairs seem an event. And the master bedroom, with its huge windows and the door leading out onto a balcony with a view, was the kind of room she had always dreamed of awakening in.

On the face of it, Roger Maxwell's own reservations seemed absurd. Why did everyone refer to the place as the Simeon King house when the old man had been dead for forty years? When they had inspected the garden, he had pointed out to Stickney an old, spreading yew whose graceless branches were mostly brown.

"That should be dug up" was all he said, and Stickney had quickly replied, "I wouldn't dare. It was planted by old Simeon himself."

I'd dare, he had thought. *If it were my place, I'd dig it out.*

The children wouldn't understand something like that. He liked older houses, but he wanted a house of his choice to be his.

Maxwell dealt with his reservation in his own way. He met with Stickney alone and offered fifteen thousand dollars below the asking price, which had been advertised as "firm." Stickney pretended dismay, but said he would pass the offer on to Mr. Searle, who at the moment was off on a spring cruise with his wife and son and daughter-in-law.

In the meantime, the Maxwells continued to inspect more conventional houses. At first the children accompanied them in order to find fault with any houses that were not the one of their choosing, but soon grew tired of trooping through other people's embarrassments. Then, one morning, there was news. Mr. Searle had been reached and had accepted the offer. Maxwell was caught by surprise, but his children's celebratory excitement convinced him that he must have made the right choice.

Of course, he had not chosen at all. They had.

The first week that the Maxwells were ensconced in their magnificent new residence, Regina realized how doll-like and sparse some of their furniture seemed. They'd need a much bigger couch before they could receive company, and they'd have to hunt around for a refectory table for the dining room. Nevertheless, she reveled in the luxury of space.

To their great good luck, Regina's advertisement in the local paper brought a call from the Sister who was acting as caretaker in a near-deserted convent; yes, they had a fourteen-foot oak table they would gladly exchange for a suitable donation. Jeb, who made friends quickly, got two of them to help load the refectory table onto a rented truck, and then the three of them got it through the French doors and into place without scratching a wall. What a surprise it was for Roger to return from work that evening and find the new table laid for dinner, a transformation that had required not a second of his own labor. How marvelous to have a growing son like Jeb!

That night at dinner, Roger wondered aloud if the preserved animals upstairs might not be deteriorating from age, and would it not be sensible to get rid of at least the two largest of them, the bear and the moose. Jeb spent his spare time during the next two days scurrying through books to find out as much about taxidermy as he could, and then informed the assembled family that Simeon King's man had done a near-perfect job and that the animals ought to be good for at least another century, if not forever.

Roger decided to name the room, as if doing so would help make the house finally his. He wanted to call it the Bestiary Room, and announced his decision to his family at dinner in the grand dining room. He tried to explain his choice, but only Regina was truly listening. The children were busy chattering about their new school, the friends they were making, and their plans for inviting old friends from their previous neighborhood to visit them for weekends to meet their new friends and to camp in that fabulous enclave upstairs, where they could horse around late into the night, away from the adult world, and then, when tiredness finally took them, they could sleep and dream.

One of the privileges Roger Maxwell reserved to himself was his solitary Sunday-morning walk, during which he reflected on the week just past and the week to come and on his own progress through life. It was during such reflective walks that he had first come to think of himself not so much as a lender of money but as a psychologist, an adviser to his business clients. They put their needs in terms of so many hundreds of thousands of dollars, but Roger understood that what they really wanted was a kind of moral support. They were entering into a gentleman's agreement that would cause his clients to do their best to bring their actual annual results as close as possible to their always optimistic projections, and that would compel him to find ways of reassuring them that his confidence remained firm, that he supported their entrepreneurial efforts and would see them through. His clients, one might say, were his children, and his role was to see them into financial adulthood.

It was on one of his early Sunday strolls that Roger met a neighbor, out walking his dog. In the chill of those spring mornings, Roger wore a sweater and sneakers and looked no more than any of his neighbors like the senior executives they all were. But the neighbor, whose name was Chalmers, turned out to be, in the course of a discussion that took them on the same course for half an hour, not an executive in industry, as Roger had first supposed, but a research scientist at the Philips Laboratories in Briarcliff. Roger had begun to be bored by the man's devotion to azaleas, and was about to find some reason to break off the conversation and go wandering back in the direction of home, when Chalmers said, "How do you like living in the Simeon King house?"

"Well," said Roger lightly, "I've come to think of it as the Maxwell house."

Out of politeness, Chalmers said, "Well, yes, of course." Then added, with a gesture of his pipe, "In fact, I've heard people saying that's the place the Maxwell kids live."

When Chalmers lifted his pipe hand in farewell as they turned the corner, Roger was lost in thought. *That house doesn't belong to Simeon King any more, it belongs to my children.*

FRIDAY

2

ONE THURSDAY EVENING in late June, Roger Maxwell went to bed right after the ten o'clock news.

"Get yourself a good night's sleep, you hear?" Regina had said.

Framed by the massive double doorway of the living room, he turned. She looked diminutive in the space of that room.

"Don't stay long," he said.

"Don't worry," she answered.

He would worry, he thought, as he climbed the stairs. They had had a nightcap together while watching the news. It was her habit to stay behind, then, after a minute's passing, go to the pantry and pour herself another vodka on the rocks, stirring it with her index finger as he had seen her do so many times. *I like to collect myself at the end of a day.* It was irrational of him to be troubled about her extra drink or two, as if her Southern background made her somehow especially susceptible to alcohol.

In bed, Roger wished she hadn't said *Get yourself a good*

night's sleep, you hear? If she had said nothing, he would have read from his bedside novel and drifted easily into sleep. But now he found himself distracted by her remark, as if it were an admonition. He had been reading the same paragraph over and over. He put the book aside and tried to think of nothing at all. Counting sheep was ridiculous. The phrase he was trying not to think of came from obituaries. *He died in his sleep.* His father had died in his sleep at fifty-three. Did that mean he had five years to go? *Ridiculous.*

Why wasn't Regina coming up? In the old house, he could hear her go to the kitchen. In this vast place, he heard nothing. If he woke tired in the morning, he'd be as disagreeable as a child without sleep. A three-day weekend lay ahead. He wanted to enjoy every minute of it.

He picked up the book again, read a page or two before a thought of obituaries intruded again. It was the damn book, of course. Everything in it seemed ominous. He put the book aside, switched off the light, and tried to make his mind a blank.

Sleep must have overtaken him, for soon Roger, in his dream, was confronting bearded Simeon King. Though photographs he had seen of the old man made him appear to be of normal height, in Roger's dream Simeon King was half again as tall as a man, and he dangled from a thumb and forefinger a foot-long key. Roger knew he had to give Simeon King the envelope—what was in it? Had he forgotten?—Money? A message? The old man nodded his approval and gave Roger the key. Roger felt a glorious joy that with this key the house he lived in was no longer the Simeon King house but *his,* and he could now cut down that spreading yew so out of place in that lower garden, and dig up the roots of that old plant he hated. The property was his own and he could do with it as he wished. The exchange was over.

Simeon had turned his back to walk away. Roger felt grateful to the old man. He put the key carefully down on a side table. He then lifted the loaded blunderbuss from the two carved duck's-head rests on the wall, aimed the weapon at Simeon's retreating back, and pulled the trigger. The explosion, as loud as the end of the world, sent the ball to strike Simeon with such force that the old man fell to the ground in fragments. Roger rushed over to examine the corpse and saw that each of the pieces was a separate child's doll, each gasping for breath, each mortally wounded, and as the dolls churned and squirmed on the ground, Roger struck the butt of the blunderbuss down at them in turn to silence their moaning as he screamed for help.

"You've had a nightmare," said Regina, standing at the bedside, fully clothed.

"What time is it?" he asked, feeling the dampness of his pajama top, drenched with sweat.

"Just midnight," she said. "I was halfway up the stairs when I heard you yelling. I thought it was—"

"A burglar."

"It could have been."

"Then you should have called the police from downstairs."

"You have the gun up here."

"It isn't loaded. You required safety at the price of security, remember?"

"Oh, Roger, I just said to keep the ammunition separate, so the children wouldn't find it. If any intruder ever gets in here, dear, I hope you'll give him what he wants and let him go."

"What if he wants you?" Roger asked.

Redressed in a fresh pajama top that Regina had held out for him to put his arms into, Roger told himself he was wrong to have snapped at her. By way of apology, he tried to put his arms around her, but she eluded him.

"I love you," she said, "but right now you need your sleep."

Out of habit, he picked up the book on his night table. *That damn thing.* He removed it to the other side of the room, where it was hidden by a pile of magazines that needed carrying to the basement. He didn't want to see it from his bed.

He heard Regina gargling in the bathroom, as she always did after brushing her teeth.

"She's right," he said to himself. "I'm impossible when I don't get a proper night's sleep."

He was thinking, I must dig out that half-dead yew by the roots. He was too tired to dig, too tired to think of anything.

When Regina came out of the bathroom in the lavender nightdress, she saw that Roger had fallen asleep with his bedside light on.

For the next eight hours Roger Maxwell slept a sleep without dreams—miraculously, it seemed to him on awaking. He felt fresh, rested, ready for the world. Sunshine streamed through the glass door to the bedroom balcony. He raised his head just enough to see 8:14 on the digital clock across the room. Oh, it was great, he had all of Friday, Saturday, and Sunday to get his mind off the bank, to do things he wanted to do, to live! Stretching his legs carefully to avoid a cramp in his calves, relishing the musculature responding to his wishes, he turned to his left to see if he was disturbing Regina or if she was still asleep.

Her side of the king-size bed was empty. He listened for the sound of the shower, thinking he might catch her there, as he had three Sundays ago, a lathery romp ending in a fervor that surprised them both.

Hearing nothing, he raised his body from the bed and went to the bathroom door. Regina's wet towel lay across the clothes hamper. *Damn, she must already be downstairs.*

In the full-length mirror, he caught the reflection of his

unmatched pajama halves and remembered the dream. He removed his pajamas, lifted Regina's wet towel, and dropped them into the hamper. In the mirror, he caught sight of his dangling appendage, looking forlorn. He laughed. God made strange body parts.

He showered, turning the water quickly to cold. He brushed his teeth, shaved, combed the hair that was still, thank heaven, thick, put on a red-and-white-striped short-sleeved sport shirt to commemorate the day off, pulled on his favorite pair of dark blue double-knit slacks, stuck his stockinged feet in comfortable Italian loafers, and went down to breakfast humming like a boy beginning summer vacation.

Regina was at the stove, her back to him. Roger inspected her tight-slacked buttocks, still his favorite part of her anatomy.

She turned, recognized the expression on his face. "You've recovered," she said. He moved to cup her behind, and caught her shrug toward Jeb and Dorry eating away at the breakfast table.

"Good morning," he announced toward the table.

"Morning," said Nancy as she came into the room and held her hands up to feel her father's face.

"You shaved."

"I did."

Sometimes Roger didn't shave till after breakfast. Nancy had made a ritual of running her palms against his cheeks to see if they were scratchy or smooth.

Pulling a chair up to the breakfast table, Roger repeated, "Good morning!"

Jeb looked up to nod, put his fork down. Dorry continued to supply thick layers of syrup-and-margarine-soaked pancake to his munching mouth until he realized that both Jeb and his father were looking at him.

"That's a nice shirt, Dad," said Jeb.

"Why, thank you," said Roger.

"It becomes you," said Regina from the stove. "It makes you look younger."

Roger laughed. "Wonder if I'd get away with a red-and-white-striped sport shirt at the bank?" *Not in this life,* he thought. "May I make a suggestion to you young wolves?"

"Sure," said Jeb.

"We should all wait till your mother sits down before we begin eating."

"Oh, Roger," said Regina, "let them while it's hot."

Dorry immediately plunged into the pancakes again.

Shop steward, he thought. *Cub defender.* "The point, Dorry," he said, "is that if you don't learn manners at home, you'll never learn them."

Dorry, his stuffed cheeks full, scowled.

Parenthood is a farce. Regina and I are just innkeepers for the children.

"Did you hear me, Dorry?"

"Coming, coming," said Regina.

Dorry put unchewed pancake from his mouth onto his fork.

"Please don't do that!" said Roger.

"I don't want any more," said Dorry.

"You should have decided that before putting it into your mouth."

"Now all of you," said Regina, bringing his plate and her own to the table. "Peace."

Roger stood to help her with her chair, but Jeb was already there. *That boy has a way with his mother.*

They all began eating except Dorry, who kept his hands in his lap.

"I think what your father is trying to tell you," said Regina to her twelve-year-old, "is that it's a sin to waste food. You should take only as much as you can eat."

"What I was saying is that it isn't very nice for the other

persons present—" he looked straight at Dorry—"if you remove food once it's in your mouth."

Dorry stood up, his chair scraping on the floor.

"Now please sit down until everyone else is finished," said Roger.

Dorry hesitated only for a moment, then fled from the room.

"You come back here!" Roger yelled after him. He could hear the boy clopping up the stairs, defiant.

Roger stood.

"Oh, leave him be," said Regina. "He'll be raiding the icebox before the morning's over."

She watched her husband go up the stairs in pursuit of the boy. "Well, they'll be down soon enough," she said to Jeb and Nancy, wishing the weekend hadn't started off this way.

Dorry was not in his room. Roger went to the usual hideout, the Bestiary. He found Dorry sitting on the elk.

"You and I are going to have a little talk," he said. "In the meantime, get off that elk."

"It's stuffed. I can't hurt it."

"Why is that pile of newspaper still in the corner there? I told you all to get rid—"

"It's Jeb's *Rolling Stones*. He says he'll kill me if I throw them out."

"I'm sure Jeb didn't use an expression like that. Now get down off that elk this minute."

Dorry slid off the elk, his feet thumping to the floor. He looked up at his father with an expression of managed innocence.

Roger felt his conscience cawing. He's only a boy. *Strictarian* was the word Regina used for him. *We are not your army.*

"Why did you leave the table, son?"

Dorry hated it when his father called him son.

"You told me not to eat."

"I said you shouldn't put food from your mouth back on the plate. Now go back down till everyone finishes."

"I'll bet . . ." said Dorry, then stopped.

"Finish any sentence you start."

"I'll bet you wish we were all stuffed like these animals."

"I am likely to die before you," said Roger, wondering where that thought had come from and why Dorry was suddenly smiling.

"I kept them hot in the oven," said Regina, putting Roger's pancakes before him.

Dorry sat grim-lipped at the table, hands folded.

Regina patted his hair. "He'll learn manners by and by," she said. "They all do."

Roger's early-morning exuberance had fled. When he was a boy, he had had to control his behavior at the table. Then he remembered the time his father had told him for the third time to stop playing with his food and to eat it, and in anger he had pulled at the tablecloth harder than he had expected and had sent his dish and silver crashing to the floor. *Children were never different.*

"Where are you?" Regina addressed his wandering mind.

"Sorry," he said, folding his napkin. "I'm afraid I need one of those damn probanthines to untie the knot in my stomach."

"I'll get it."

"No, you've got your own break—" But she was gone.

"Jeb?"

His sixteen-year-old looked up at him.

Roger spoke in his most controlled voice, reasonable and calm. "I hope you're planning to cut the lawn today, Jeb."

"I was planning," said Jeb, watching his father's face, "to cut it Sunday afternoon."

"It needs cutting at the beginning of a weekend, not the end. It's almost as long as your hair," said Roger, sorry the moment the words were out of his mouth. He had promised Regina to stop about the hair.

He wants the lawn to look like his hair, thought Jeb.

"Jeb, you know that if you cut off more than a third, it hurts the grass. It's already too long."

"Dad?" said Jeb.

Roger thought the boy's voice sounded conciliatory. "Yes?"

"You're staying home today?"

"I am."

"Wouldn't the exercise be good for you?"

"What exercise?" asked Roger, taking the proffered pill from Regina and, with a swallow of coffee, downing it.

"Cutting the lawn," said Jeb. "I thought you might *like* to do it."

Roger carefully buttered his pancakes in silence. Then he said, "I wasn't expecting to spend a vacation day doing the lawn with an expert like you around."

"I was going over to Donald's house," said Jeb.

"Walking the mower around the lawn is shorter than walking over to Donald's. It'll take less time."

"I was going to borrow the station wagon."

"I thought Donald was coming here for the weekend." Roger looked over at Regina for help.

"That's this evening. I have an appointment."

"A what?"

"To go over to his place after breakfast."

"To do what?" said Roger, wishing his voice wouldn't rise so.

"Fool around."

"What's that mean?"

Jeb scraped his plate with his fork.

"Don't *do* that," said Regina. "Please!"

"I suggest you fool around with the grass first," said Roger.

Jeb looked at his mother, hoping for help.

Regina's lips, as imperceptibly as possible, formed the words: *You do the grass.* Out loud she said, "Get it done and it'll be out of the way." Then to Roger she said, "Louise wants to talk to us after breakfast."

"Oh, no," said Roger. "I hope it's not one of those I'm-quitting-unless sermons."

"I'm sure you'll charm her as always, dear."

Crazy to have to be liked by your servants, thought Roger. It's all upside down.

"I've got to call Cargill first," said Roger.

"Can't you call him Monday morning?"

"When he called yesterday, my secretary told him I was in an all-day meeting and would be taking a long weekend, and he said if I wasn't going to be in on Friday, I should call."

"I just hate the idea of you talking business on a weekend, dear."

Jeb and Dorry, as if by prearranged signal, got up.

"Sit down till your father finishes," Regina ordered them. "Roger, you've barely touched your pancakes. Get out of bed the wrong side this morning?"

I got out of the bed when you weren't in it, Roger thought.

"Why do you have to call Mr. Cargill?" asked Jeb, the voice of rationality.

Because Cargill's account is too important to ignore, whatever the day of the week, he thought. He said, "Jeb, it's only polite to return a call from someone I've known as long as Mr. Cargill. He might need help."

Why do children know when you're lying?

"What's this mob we've got staying over the weekend?" he asked.

"Dorry's having Kenny and Mike," said Regina. "They're both nice boys. He's stayed over at Kenny's already. And Nancy's having Bernice, and Jeb's got Donald and—what's his name? Might as well have them all at once."

"His name," said Jeb, "is not what's-his-name. It's El Greco. You've met him."

"Is that his real name?" asked Roger.

"Oh, Roger," said Regina, "that couldn't be his real name."

"Is he Greek?" Roger asked Jeb.

"He's black. You remember him, Mom."

Regina remembered him. When Jeb had first brought him around, she wondered whether her son ought to have a friend who was at least three years older, surely nineteen, and drove a car of his own. And why shouldn't he have a car? She assumed that because his parents were black they could not afford to give him a car. Where had he earned the money? Was she uneasy because she didn't want Jeb associating with a boy who did not go on to college? Or were all these apprehensions merely decorations of her mind, covering her real concern, his color? Regina had decided that she had insufficiently mastered the prejudices of her childhood. El Greco was Jeb's friend and that was enough.

"Why is he called El Greco?" Roger was saying. "Does he paint? Is he artistic?"

"He's got rhythm, Dad," said Jeb.

Regina laughed.

Roger, trapped in a conversation he saw no way out of, pushed his plate three inches forward.

Nancy, still eating, stopped.

"I'll go call Cargill," Roger said.

"Don't forget Louise wants a conversation with us."

At the door, Roger said to Jeb, "Don't forget to mow the lawn."

Jeb raised a middle finger at Roger's departed back. Dorry and Nancy giggled. Regina slapped at the raised finger. "He's your father!"

"Are you sure?" said Jeb.

"You are impudent!"

"Everything I am I learned at home," said Jeb, one hand mock held over his sixteen-year-old heart.

"I hope I'm not phoning too early, Bill," said Roger.

"Not at all," said Cargill. "I was hoping to get together with you late in the day yesterday, but your secretary said you were in a meeting she couldn't break into."

"What's up?" asked Roger, immediately sensing the abruptness of his question. "Any problem I can help with?"

Cargill was silent for a moment. "I think we should probably get together for a chat."

"Monday?"

"I may be committed by the end of Monday."

Committed to what? Roger thought. *I don't belong to you today. This is my day off.* He said, "I've got to have a word with the damn housekeeper before she goes into town, but I could drive over before noon."

"I don't want to put you to any trouble," said Cargill, "especially since you've elected a holiday today. I'm taking off for the Tarrytown Marina momentarily. You're up that way, aren't you?"

"A bit farther north."

"That's all right. Why don't I stop by?"

"Sure." He gave Cargill directions, then said, "Bill, don't keep me in suspense. What's it about?"

"About two and a half million dollars," said Cargill, laughing. "See you soon."

When he'd hung up, Maxwell thought *that's exactly his present line of credit, and he's not using all of it. Why the hurry?*

In the Bestiary, Jeb, sixteen-year-old caliph, lay stretched on an upper-level bunk bed, fingers twined on chest.

"Dorry!" Jeb's command filled the room. The animals, unmoved, kept silent.

Dorry, minor caliph on the bunk below, said, "Now what?"

"Get me that."

"Get you what?"

"I'm pointing."

"How'm I supposed to see from here?"

"Get your ass out of the bunk and you'll see what I'm pointing at."

Dorry, knowing the order of the world, slid out of the bunk.

"That," said Jeb, pointing at the pile of *Rolling Stones.*

"Which one?" said Dorry.

"Don't be dumb. The top one."

Dorry stood on the lower bunk, handed the magazine up, watched his brother put the magazine beside him and refold his hands.

"Aren't you going to read it?" asked Dorry.

"I read it."

"What'd you make me get it for?"

Unanswered, Dorry slid into the lower bunk, resigned to his station.

Generalissimo Jeb surveyed his domain. Postered walls. Animals in place.

The bear wore its new red paper Hawaiian lei well. The garland's parabola framed four round slogan buttons pinned like medals on the fur.

Jeb laughed. The jockstrap on the bear had been his idea, too.

"We ought to have a lock on the door," said Jeb.

"What for?" said Dorry.

"What for? What for?" Jeb shrill-mimicked his brother's changing voice. "There's a lock on the bathroom door, isn't there?"

"Mom wouldn't like it."

"Mom wouldn't like it." Then, "You getting hairs?"

"What do you mean?" said Dorry quietly.

"You know what I mean."

"You saw. I know you saw."

"Three hairs isn't hair," said Jeb.

"More'n three."

"Four?" Jeb laughed a caliph-sneer.

"More'n four. Lots."

"Let me see."

"What for?"

Jeb took note of the tremor in his brother's voice. Putting his hands behind his head, he let a moment's silence work its damage. "Still bite your nails?"

"Mom says you used to bite your nails," said Dorry.

"How many nails you got?"

"Ten."

"Don't you have nails on your feet?"

"Ten on my hands."

"You're stupid. How'd you like nine on your hands? Get me my pliers from downstairs."

"I didn't *do* anything."

Dorry's head turned at the small, saving knock on the Bestiary Room door, quickly followed by a second.

"Who's there?" said Jeb. "This is a private room."

"Mommy," said a girl's voice. The doorknob turned, in came Nancy, tongue out at caliph Jeb. With her was a shorter girl, swinging loose-hanging hair her mother brushed once in the morning, once at night.

"Bernice came early," Nancy said.

"Hi, Bernice," said Dorry, saved.

Bernice was shy of speech. She thought of herself as a store-window dummy waiting to be dressed, wearing nothing but hair. She was crushingly in love with Nancy, who knew she was not just a hank of hair.

"Shut the door," Jeb ordered.

"Do like he says," said Dorry, trying for Jeb's resonance.

"What's that you got on the bear?" asked Nancy.

"A jockstrap, dope. Want him to get a hernia?"

"I mean the red thing around his neck," said Nancy.

"Don't tear it!" said Jeb.

"I'm just looking."

"It's a lei," said Dorry, smirking.

Both girls giggled at the word.

"You interrupted," said Jeb. "I was just going to operate on Dorry."

"No, you weren't," said Dorry.

"Just a fingernail," said Jeb casually. "You, Bernice, say hello."

Bernice squeezed a whispered salutation from her mouth. "Hello."

Jeb swung himself upright on the bunk. "Can you read?" addressing Bernice.

"Course she can read," said Nancy.

"Read the first button," ordered Jeb.

Bernice short-stepped to the bear, the button higher than her eyes. "It says . . ."

She giggled.

"Giggle, giggle, giggle," said Jeb. "Read!"

Sober, slack-faced, Bernice read. "Kiss me, I can't stand it."

"You heard her," Jeb bellowed at Dorry on the bunk below. "Obey!"

"I don't want him to kiss me," said Bernice.

"I heard you the first time," said Jeb. "Dorry!"

Red-faced Dorry slunk from the bed, advanced on his victim.

Bernice stepped backward.

With one bound, Jeb leaped from the top bunk, feet thudding the floor, grabbed Bernice's hands, and putting each hand on the bear's chest, said, "You move your hands on pain of death, understand? Nancy, you go there." He pointed her away to a corner of the room. "Now, Dorry, do as she said."

"Do I have to?"

"Get me the pliers then."

"Okay, okay."

Cautiously, Dorry approached the frightened girl.

"She's my guest," said Nancy.

"You shut up," said Jeb.

Dorry awkwardly put his face over Bernice's stretched left arm, quick-pecked her cheek.

"That's no kiss," said Jeb. "On the lips."

"No," said Bernice.

"Don't you move your hands!"

"I'm not moving my hands."

"Okay, Dorry. Go."

Scrunching his head into his shoulders, Dorry wet his lips.

"Don't move!" said Jeb

Dorry stopped.

"I meant Bernice."

Dorry reached his head out from the sanctuary of his shoulders, kissed Bernice's lips.

"That's better," said Jeb smiling. "Don't move."

Gruffly, he pushed Dorry out of the way.

Nancy, fascinated, watched her immobilized friend.

"What color are they?" Jeb asked.

"Are what?" whispered Bernice.

"Your panties."

Bernice wrenched her head toward the corner where Nancy hovered. her eyes pleading help.

"I said what color?"

A whisper. "White."

"How do I know you're telling the truth. Dorry," Jeb hurled his voice at his brother, "check that out."

Dorry sidled over to Bernice.

"What are you scared of?" Jeb said. "Didn't you ever play doctor? I know *you* played doctor, Nancy. Didn't you, Bernice?"

Bernice's blue-white lips were bitten inward. Dorry and Jeb both heard the squish, saw the shock on Bernice's face as. hands still outstretched against the bear, urine ran down her leg.

"Now you'll *have* to take your panties off," said Jeb.

As if breaking from a magnetic field, Bernice pulled her hands free from the bear and ran across the room to Nancy, burying her face in Nancy's shoulder, just as the door opened and Regina, taking in the two boys, the huddled girls, said, "What's going on here?"

Jeb's tyrannous gaze speared across the room at Nancy.

"Nothing," said Nancy.

"Well, Jeb," said Regina, "you'd better go cut the grass right now."

Outside, the lawn mower provided background noise as Louise sat opposite Roger and Regina, her hands lap-folded, a bundle of too many clothes over her fifty years of shapelessness. She talked, as usual, in interrogatories.

"You know my father was a minister?"

"Yes, Louise, you told us when we hired you."

"You know my husband also was a minister?"

"Yes, Louise."

"I forgave him when he ran away with that woman. He needed sex badly." She touched her embroidered handkerchief to the edge of her right eye. "I hope you don't mind my being personal?"

"Go right ahead, dear," said Regina, thinking she should not have said dear.

"I am a God-fearing woman," said Louise.

Roger wished she would get on with it. She had obviously rehearsed what she wanted to say in a certain order, and if she lost her way, she would be upset, and more difficult to deal with.

"About that upstairs room."

"The Bestiary?" asked Regina.

"Mrs. Maxwell, you know the room I am referring to. I don't think God made animals for stuffing. I won't touch those creatures."

"Louise," Roger said, "we didn't stuff those animals."

"Oh, I know that!"

"The house came that way from its previous owner."

"Why keep them? It's like a zoo."

"Well," Roger lied, "we were just talking the other day about giving them away."

"It's just that the children enjoy them so," said Regina.

"I can't clean that room." She shifted her weight. "I don't ever want to go into that room. It's my religious upbringing."

"We can get a cleaning service in once a month to deal with that room," said Roger.

"And I'd be happy to change the bunk bed sheets myself," said Regina.

Louise seemed relieved. "I was going to quit, you know."

"We hoped you wouldn't," said Regina. "We've enjoyed having you with the family."

"I'm going into town for the weekend, since you're all

home. You know my friend, Arista, the one I stay with when I'm in town, she set up for me to see her minister, which I'm doing late this afternoon. I want to consult with him, you understand, about those animals. It's not just the cleaning, it's living under one roof with them. I want to find out what the minister thinks."

"You'll let us know, won't you?" said Regina.

"Sunday night. I had a letter from my husband, by the way."

"I remember you getting a forwarded letter."

"He says he's enjoying his new life real well. He means sex, of course, though he didn't say it outright like that. He said he hopes I'm enjoying my new life. He sent a small check, which is nice. I haven't told him about the animals. I'm expecting to write soon."

Roger felt as if he hadn't been dismissed yet. "I hope you have a good time this weekend in town," he said. "I'd be happy to give you a ride to the station."

"I prefer the exercise. I like to walk about. I have walked every street in this new neighborhood, up driveways, too, getting vibrations from the houses. I wouldn't say this was a very religious community."

Roger turned to his wife for help.

"Louise," said Regina, "I'm glad you were frank with us. About your feelings. We respect them."

"Thank you, Mrs. Maxwell." she stood.

Roger fled to the out-of-doors.

Outside, he saw that about one-third of the grass had been cut. The mower had been abandoned in mid-strip. Jeb was nowhere in sight. The partly shorn lawn looked terrible. Cargill should be here momentarily. Walking fast, Roger went around behind the house. The station wagon was gone.

He could have throttled Jeb.

3

WHEN MAXWELL HEARD Cargill's car on the gravel driveway, he dropped his newspaper without taking time to fold it and with a brisk pace walked around the north side of the house, slowing down as he turned the corner so as not to seem to be hurrying.

Dorry and Nancy, forever dashing to greet newcomers, were already at the side of the white convertible, saying hello to Cargill and to the attractive, red-haired woman beside him, while Bernice hung back bashfully like a stick.

"What're your names?" Cargill was saying to the kids, then, over Dorry's shoulder, "Hi, Roger, come meet Anthea."

Cargill, in his late thirties, seemed younger, decked in a fine tan, topped by a captain's cap, and uniformed in an Italian sailor shirt and white duck slacks, looking more like imitation Gatsby than someone who would pass at the Yacht Club in New York.

He always had an attractive woman with him. More than

once when Cargill had had a drink with Roger in town to discuss a point after hours, he would be joined at some precise time by a date whom he would introduce with something like, "This is So-and-So—remember the girl I told you I was having an affair with?" The women seemed to enjoy his directness. Roger remembered when Cargill, early in their acquaintance, nearly ten years ago, said, "I guess a banker couldn't live the way I do, could he? Propriety's a helluva burden. I fornicate, commit adultery, I even drive women across state lines, while you've got to look like those pillars in the bank, upright and polished at all times. Never mind, Roger, I envy the stability in your life," and he had laughed uproariously. At times, when Regina kept to herself, Roger envied Cargill his varied sexual partners.

"Well, what are your names? Mine's Bill Cargill. I'm a friend of your father's."

Nancy wasn't sure Mr. Cargill really wanted her to answer. "My name's Nancy," she said anyway.

"What about you, Buster?" said Cargill to Dorry.

"Theodore." He blushed. "But everybody calls me Dorry."

"You can call me Uncle Bill if you want to. Hey, Roger, these are nice kids."

Having clients you depend on, thought Roger, *is like having servants you depend on. Such an effort to pretend all the time.*

Roger leaned over the woman's side of the car and shook her hand. It was warm and had a graceful shape. But his eyes held to her flaring hair, not auburn but real red, cascading about her face, wind-blown from the ride. If it were Regina, she'd be fixing it. This woman didn't care. He wished Regina wouldn't care.

"Anthea," said Cargill, sliding out from behind the wheel, "move over. Roger and I are going to be talking a—what?— hour or so? Take a ride. There's some terrific views around here over by the river " And when he saw her moving over to the driver's side, he said, "Okay, Roger, let's find ourselves a quiet place. You lead." He waved to Anthea as she drove off.

Roger took Cargill on an inspection tour of the out-of-doors.

"Nice pool you got," said Cargill. "I never keep a place long enough to build a pool and I never found a place I liked that already had one. By the way, your directions were terrific. When you told me the turn was five point three miles, I had to keep from laughing, but damn if it wasn't bop on the head. Say, I see I caught you in the middle of doing your lawn."

"No, no," Roger said quickly. "One of my sons. He'll finish it after our talk. We don't need the noise.

"Let me show you the living room," said Roger, opening the terrace doors. Sensing Cargill's reluctance, he added, "It'll just take a minute."

Inside, Cargill gazed at the spacious, elegant room.

"Pretty fancy," he said.

Did Cargill think the banker who served him should live in more modest circumstances?

They settled on the terrace, where Regina brought them both coffee.

"Milk and sugar?" she asked.

"Tell you what, Mrs. Maxwell, what I'd really like is a squirt of brandy in it, just a drop. Is that okay?"

Cargill's eyes followed Regina into the house. "That is a well-built woman you've got, especially—"

He had stopped himself, but Roger had seen the direction of his examination.

This man, Roger thought, *would fuck my wife, given half a chance.*

"Sailing today?" he asked, addressing himself to the maritime garb.

"Sleeps two real comfortably," Cargill said. "And I tell you, Roger old man, the purr of those engines is one of the best aphrodisiacs made."

The boat had been added to Cargill's personal financial statement the last time it was redone for the bank. He'd been a boy wonder in his twenties, just beginning to cash in, when Roger had gotten his account. Despite bank policy of moving loan officers about every few years, Roger had managed to keep Cargill all the way, fascinated by the man's ingenious entrepreneurship. Cargill's idea had been that most men who bought in hardware stores were do-it-yourselfers, tools and gadgets were their toys, and so he set up a supersized hardware store in a way that made every wall and aisle a museum-of-science-and-industry display, so you could try things out. The signs said TRY IT, not HANDS OFF. It was the kind of shop a man could wander around in, enjoy, and be tempted to buy things he might not need but could find some use for if he had them at home. "Shopping is sightseeing," Cargill would say. Nothing was hidden in cabinets except reserve stock. Cargill's sales per square foot of space proved to be four hundred per-cent higher than the average for hardware stores that catered to necessity rather than temptation. He quickly converted the success of one store into a chain of Cargill's Hardware Super-markets, located them mainly in the new shopping centers, preferably between the men's clothing store and the liquor store, to catch them coming and going. Now there were one hundred forty-three Hardware Supermarkets scattered about the eastern seaboard, and a month didn't pass without another being added, but in some ways it was still a personal business. Cargill himself had the final say in hiring each new manager. He once told Roger, "I can smell if a man is good."

Cargill's account at the bank usually had a minimal float. That man really watched his pennies. No hired manager would do that. He always let Maxwell pick up the check at lunch, never even made a pass at reciprocity. Cargill himself was into municipals long before they became popular for less than the very rich. He not only enjoyed the tax-free income but also reveled in the idea that the federal and state governments would get no part of what was earned by the money he was able to put aside.

"Honestly," Cargill said, once the brandy had been made available and Regina had vanished into the house, "I'd rather have had this talk in the office." His eyes examined Maxwell to ascertain his mood. "I have a problem. Or you've got a problem. Depends."

"Well why don't you relax and tell me about it. You haven't come anywhere near using your full line—"

"That's not it," said Cargill. "If I'd need a bigger line, I know you'd give it to me. Cash flow's okay, but with stores building all the time, it's not always going to be. My problem is the *cost* of cash."

"I thought you were happy with half a point above prime."

"Oh, I was, I was," said Cargill, on his feet, restlessly biting off the end of a cigar, leaning over Maxwell for the proffered light. "But then this guy from First National City gets to me—I mean I couldn't turn down his request for an interview, could I?—and he says they're interested in my concept, think the chain has national possibilities. Anyway"—he was pacing now, stopped to look at Maxwell—"he offered prime."

Roger had to think. The Review Board discussed every account that closed. When it was a big account, you had to pin it on somebody. Nobody ever got fired from the bank, but they could sure kill you while you were still living.

"Well," Roger said, exhaling. "I didn't know you were in a league with General Motors, Bill."

"I'm not. They just want the account."

"Bill, I'm awfully glad you see that. They can promise you prime, give you prime. What happens if a few of the new stores don't work out, profit dips, cash is tough? What's to keep them from charging you half a point or maybe a whole point over prime six months from now, a year from now?"

"Nothing. I'd move back to you or anywhere else that'd have me. Right now they're talking of saving me ten grand hard cash on what I'm using currently. That's money found. Profit. Look, Roger, suppose I decide to sell out someday, suppose at that point my line at the bank is—what?—twice what I've got now? If I'm at prime, that's a saving of over twenty thousand of pretax net. If I get a ten multiple from some conglomerate, that's one hundred thousand extra in my pocket if I save the half a point now and keep it that way."

The man's a penny pincher. He's not a gentleman. Roger caught his own lie. *He's a son of a bitch because he understands. I like accounts that treat the bank with respect, not as if it was a Persian marketplace for money.* Still a lie. *I want compliant accounts. Obedient accounts. This man resents the size of the house I live in. He thinks I make too much money. He's getting even.*

"What do you think?" Cargill's cigar was pointing at him. *Save the account. Don't score points.*

Roger's voice was calm. "I've always thought that what counts with a banking arrangement is not the rate but the relationship. We know you. You know us. We've brought you along. I remember when your line was fifty thousand dollars, not two and a half million. Your business grew with our money because we had confidence in what you were doing. If you had problems, we'd be there."

"You're not trying to sell me on sentiment, Roger? I'm a big boy."

"I'm reminding you that you have a substantial asset in our relationship."

"Ten thousand dollars cash right now, a value of twenty times that later."

Roger's heart thumped in a way he hoped didn't show. "What do you want me to do?"

"I wasn't expecting you just to say good-bye." Cargill smiled. "Match it."

"Prime?"

"Prime."

"My committee would never buy it."

"I'm sure you can sell it to them."

"They'd see it as a bad precedent."

Cargill examined the end of his cigar. "Who has to know? It's between me and the bank."

"That's not how bankers think."

"I know you, Roger," Cargill said. "You're not hidebound like the others. The bank makes a profit at prime. You want to play along."

Roger wished Cargill wasn't leaning so close to him.

"Yes," he said. "However, it comes at an inconvenient time for me."

"I'm sorry about that."

"When must you know?"

"Tuesday."

"That's very soon."

"That's why I tried to get you yesterday. That's why I stopped by here today. They don't want their offer hanging around. It was their deadline, not mine."

Roger doubted that. Cargill had organized the pressure.

They both heard the sound of the car in the driveway. "She's back," said Cargill. "Gotta go."

He held out his hand. "Whatever happens," he said, "I know we'll still be friends."

We were never friends, thought Roger.

Even before Cargill's car was out of the driveway, Roger had started the lawn mower up and was pushing it down the unfinished row, cutting the seeded heads off the long grass, the grass bag filling up rapidly, just as he had with anger.

Forty minutes later, his red-and-white sport shirt drenched in sweat, Roger had rehearsed and rehearsed an imaginary meeting of the committee in his head, and saw no way of convincing them to give a business like Cargill's the prime rate. They'd laugh at him if he persisted. When the cash crunch was on in late 1966, the committee had wanted Cargill to clean up early. They had pretended to be worried about Cargill's liquidity. It was just the fucking money they wanted. And he had saved the son of a bitch. Cargill had no loyalty. Look at the way he flitted from woman to woman.

Roger was nearly finished with the lawn when he heard the voice trying to get through behind him. He turned the lawn-mower engine down.

"Hi, Dad," said Jeb. "Want me to finish?"

"It's almost finished, can't you see!"

"I'll do it."

Roger turned the lawn-mower engine up, but Jeb just stood there.

"What do you want now?" Roger shouted above the noise.

"Could I . . ." The boy's voice was as loud as his own, a man's voice. "The yew," Jeb shouted, "the one you wanted to dig out of the lower garden, can I do that for you?"

"No!" Roger snapped. "I'll do that myself!"

"I'm just trying to help."

"You go to hell!"

Jeb looked as if he had been struck. He stood stock still a second, then lumbered away like a wounded giraffe.

Roger wanted to call him back. How could he explain that he had to dig out Simeon's yew himself? Or that Cargill's ultimatum was the spur of his anger? It wasn't Jeb's fault. He wasn't being fair!

4

AS ROGER GUIDED the lawn mower down the last row of uncut grass, he thought of what Regina always referred to as "Roger's album," although it wasn't his. It was a family album of which only the plan was of his devising. The album was divided into four sections, labeled for each of the children, each section beginning with the inane photo taken of the child in the hospital within days of its birth—pictures the children would have preferred destroyed. The hospital photo was followed by a snapshot taken each year on the child's birthday. Thus far, the chain of photos was unbroken. Keeping the ritual, he felt, somehow protected the lives of his children. *If a child died, you couldn't add the birthday photo. Therefore, if you added a photo, it meant that child could not die.* Once he had had to be abroad on an unavoidable business trip when Harry was turning four, and Regina had dutifully taken the snapshot, a bit out of focus—she said Harry had moved. Harry, in later years, said it had probably been Mother's hands shaking because of the responsibility of taking the picture for Dad's album.

Roger turned the mower off and went to his study, where the album was kept in the lower right-hand drawer of his desk. He didn't know why he still felt furtive when glancing through its pages, the way he had as a boy looking at forbidden books. There was Harry, right through his twentieth birthday, though for the last couple of years Harry had protested mildly that the process could not be kept up, what with him away at school.

In raising Harry, he had told Regina he hoped for the best possible compromise, the maximum of desirable traits with a minimum of the kinds of trouble children and teen-agers get into. It was only a couple of years ago that Roger realized how Harry's talent for handling his peers and adults with seeming grace and effortless conciliation was really a self-serving skill, allowing each person a moment on stage only when Ringmaster Harry called the turns. However diplomatic his manner, he used people, including his parents, until one day Roger made it clear he did not wish to be manipulated any more by his son. Harry didn't seem bothered. The world was full of people waiting for his polite instruction.

Roger turned to Jeb's pages in the album. In life he had turned from his close bond with Harry to Jeb, hoping that Jeb would not disappoint him as Harry had. Jeb from the age of ten or eleven seemed the opposite of Harry. While Harry, under his self-effacing manner, used others as chess pieces with the confidence that he would one day be a grand master of people, Jeb spoke his mind without thought of the consequences. Or at least so Roger thought until Jeb was twelve, when he realized that Jeb's candor was really a challenge to others to love him despite his lack of diplomacy. Jeb couldn't rival Harry at Harry's game, so he constructed his own rules.

From the moment that Roger had realized this, Jeb had become his secret favorite. Roger saved loving compliments for Jeb, treating his rebellious forthrightness as if it was expected. And the result was, of course, that Jeb found himself forced to devise ever more stinging comments to test his father's love.

On one occasion, Jeb had turned down Roger's invitation to a father-and-son outing in favor of a friend's party. Roger had said, "Never mind, it's okay," but he, in his hurt, had decided to protect himself by building a stronger relationship with Dorry, who was then at the very age that Jeb had been when Roger had felt closest to him. However, Roger was also tempted by the attractions of Nancy, who idolized her father, and seemed, at this moment of her life, totally without guile. Roger saw the process: he was an increasingly dispensable parent to each of his children in turn.

Flipping back to Jeb's pages in the album, he regretted the words he could not shake from his mind: *You go to hell!* He would have to remedy that quickly.

Roger failed to sense Regina's presence until she put her arm through his, her skin touching his skin.

"So this is where you've been hiding," she said.

Embarrassed, Roger slipped the album into the open drawer. "I've got to put the lawn mower away," he said.

"Do it later," she said.

"I haven't done the edges. You know how the grass looks when the edges are ragged."

"Jeb can do that. Why don't you come for a walk with me?"

How could he refuse her? At that moment, she seemed more than beautiful, radiating a sense of joyful confidence, a woman in whose company he longed to spend whatever was yet allotted to him in life.

She led him outside, and they strolled. Regina guided him from the gravel walk onto the lawn, away from the house.

"How did your talk with Cargill go?" Her voice had a lilt to match the spring of her step.

Roger's free hand made a short, dismissive gesture in the air. No point in passing the worry to her. He said, "I hope you noticed Cargill's appreciative eye for you."

"Nostalgia for an older generation whose women made few demands. He's quite a swordsman, isn't he? Well, never mind, hippity-hop, down one rabbit hole, up another." She swayed as they walked arm in arm along the lawn's perimeter. "Do you envy men who chase young bodies?"

"Madame," said Roger, "I cultivate amorous accomplishment, not young ladies hoping for a second date."

He felt an appreciative pressure on his arm.

"Experience is one thing, taut skin another," she said, as if it were a question.

"Madame, your skin is as beautiful as the day you first let me cast my eyes on all of it."

She touched her finger to the bud of a rose. "Why, Mr. Maxwell," she said, "that's enough to make a lady blush."

She removed her arm from his and slipped her hand to his buttock. Roger instinctively glanced around. Regina laughed. "Roger, Mother and Father are no longer watching us."

"The children—" he began.

"Are quite capable of withstanding the shock of seeing some affection pass between their parents, would you not agree?"

He laughed.

"Mr. Maxwell, suh," she said, honey in her voice, "do you all yearn sometimes for a Southern bride with one orifice mysteriously sealed?"

"I'll bet you were an uninhibited adventuress when you were as young as Nancy is now." *He remembered how shy she had been.*

"I declare," she said, mocking the accent Southern ladies affected in the movies, "a woman my age can barely remember being a virgin." Suddenly she bent her head, relishing his embarrassment as she darted her tongue in his ear and ran off, stopping only to kick off her sandals and make sure he was following, then sped across the lawn, breathless, stumbling, when it was possible for him to catch up to her.

Roger held her firmly by both her arms.

"Why, Mr. Maxwell, you wouldn't dream of taking a lady by force?" She allowed herself to sink to the grass, Roger not letting go. He was kissing her when they both heard the voice from a window of the house.

It was Dorry yelling, "Mom, are you busy?"

Regina stood up, her hands on her hips, and shouted, "We are making love!"

Dorry's face at the window vanished, and the casement shut.

"You see," she said, lying down beside Roger, "it couldn't have been important."

Roger, his fingers interlocked behind his head, watched the clouds, pale smoke puffs against the brilliant blue of a clear sky. "I envy you," he said.

"How?"

"You make privacy anywhere. You're not embarrassed."

"You were born wearing a vest. I think that's why you became a banker. It gave you a profession to hide behind."

Roger knew she would have preferred him to pursue a romantic career, something in the arts, or exercising his intellect. He would have been the same but they would have had different friends, she had once said. Yet, perhaps he would not have been the same.

"I could have been a cardboard-box manufacturer," he said.

"Or a politician," she said.

"No. One has to draw the line somewhere."

"How about here." With a finger she traced a line down

the side of his face, across his chest on a diagonal, then, at an angle, lower, causing him to turn his body toward the grass. "Children could be watching."

"Fuck the children," Regina said, and he loved her for it.

They lay for a time side by side watching the sky, their thoughts separating.

After a while, Regina said, "While you and Mr. Wandering Eye were having your busy-busy-busy, I was kitchening away when the phone rang. I picked it up and, before I could say hello or anything, I could hear Dorry on the extension.

"And you listened in."

"I am not without sin." She squeezed his arm. "It was Matilda asking for Jeb. Jeb was at Donald's, so she left a curious message. Tell Jeb it's okay for tonight."

"I thought Jeb had his friends staying overnight."

"I wonder what our sixteen-year-old is up to."

"I wish I knew," said Roger, but his thoughts had fled elsewhere, trying to formulate a way to put a prime rate request before the committee on Monday without sounding like a damn fool.

"Roger Maxwell, you are not listening to me."

He put his arm across her and kissed her perfunctorily.

"Now you just get your mind back here where it belongs," Regina said, and this time she kissed him, her lips just brushing his lips.

Roger imagined Cargill standing at the edge of a cliff. Roger pushed, and Cargill went flying over the edge. He liked that better than the way he had got rid of Simeon King.

"Why are you laughing?" Regina asked.

"Getting rid of an intruder," he said, taking her face that he loved into both his hands and raising her head to his, their mouths together, her scent an aphrodisiac that belonged only to her except for those moments, like this, when he was allowed to share it.

"Why, thank you," she said, gasping for breath, her accent suddenly deeply Southern, as it sometimes became when they were loving each other as they did in the very early days of their wild unbearable agonizing infatuation.

Why, thank you is what she said from time to time as the tremors of her orgasm quieted enough for normal speech. The first time she had screamed during an orgasm, he remembered, he had been frightened beyond belief, fearing he had penetrated the vagina wall. *No, no,* she had gasped as he withdrew, *stay there.* That scream had made her shyness fly, never to return. For a time she became a bobcat, her nail marks drawing blood on his back, and when he lay back, wounded yet still erect, she had mounted and ridden him, the aureoles of her breasts above him flushed, a vein standing out. Beautiful and swaying, she had peaked, then fell exhausted across him, kissing his nipples, biting to make him forget his back, and afterward standing up naked, her hands on her hips so that he could admire a full view of her, saying, "Well, Roger, if Southern ladies don't behave this way, I guess I just ain't."

"What are you remembering?" she asked now on the grass, and he whispered the word they both used as a code for that remembered occasion.

She got up from the grass and took his hand and led him to the house. Happily, they encountered none of the children. Up the grand staircase to their bedroom, they let their clasped hands sway backward once or twice. When their hands touched his groin as if by accident, it excited him the way it had when, as a young officer in the army, he had been sitting at the bar of a cocktail lounge and a woman he didn't know sat next to him and, without a word, let her hand drop to his lap. She had said "Excuse me" but had not removed her hand, and that, too, had taught him the value of surprise.

Locked in their room, Regina turned her back and dropped her slacks so that his favorite portion of her anatomy would be in view even before she removed her blouse, which she now did, as Roger said, "No wonder it looked so good when you were bending over the stove at breakfast." She was not wearing anything under her slacks. *Regina is a devil,* he marveled to himself as she undressed him.

At six in the evening, Regina reported that all the weekend children had arrived and were gathered in the Bestiary Room, listening to music that from two floors below sounded like the rumble of bad weather.

"Food's ready," said Regina. "Want me to get them?"

"I'll do it," said Roger.

"We want all the time we can get before dark," she said. "Hurry."

On the third floor, Roger's hand gripped the cold round knob. He pushed open the Bestiary Room door, his last protection from the blast of rock that assaulted his ears. *Throw a hand grenade into the enemy room, quick slam the door shut: lesson of war.*

Through the drifts of smoke, eight faces watched the intruder. From their places the stuffed animals glared. On the walls, new posters. Obscene, thick-lipped black Hendrix strumfucking his guitar—wasn't he dead? Joplin's lips ready to suck the microphone head—wasn't she dead? What was it with children now? He wanted to shout *shut up* through the din. Nancy and her friend Bernice huddled on a lower bunk; how could they be talking in all that noise? What were those three d ing Dorry and his new slave-friend Kenny and that boy Mike? Were they laughing at him? El Greco mock-dancing the brown bear, Donald clapping, Jeb clapping. *What the hell was going on?*

Nothing?

Jeb lifted the needle from the record. Silence cut the room

in two, the children and the animals on one side, Roger Maxwell frozen at the door.

"Hi, Dad," said Jeb. "Anything wrong?"

They were kids, the intruder told himself.

"Winded from the stairs," said Roger.

All eight faces watched him.

Get ahold of yourself. You are polite to clients. Be polite to children's friends. Make your face smile. His voice invaded the silence.

"You are all welcome," he said. "Just remember there are two adult residents in this household who are also hoping for some rest this weekend."

When he had lectured recruits during the war, he'd radar-sweep their eyes, searching for anyone not listening.

"Please let us all cooperate. If you follow instructions, we'll have a good time at Echo Lake this evening, and for the rest of the weekend, too. We're all set to leave now, the food is in baskets, we'll eat as soon as we get there, and then you're free to roam the place—staying out of mischief—until dark, when we'll reassemble for the drive back home. Any questions?"

It was only then that he saw Regina in the open door. *Mr. Pompous-ass,* she had once called him when she caught him lecturing the kids. *They are not your troops.*

"The treat I've prepared for the master of the household," she said, "won't stay hot forever, so shall we go?"

There was rumbled approval from the children. And then they all thundered down the stairs in a picnic mood, deserting the animals in the Bestiary.

Roger went last, turning out the lights and making sure the doors were locked. Outside, they assembled in front of the beleaguered station wagon, which seemed too small to accommodate them all.

"No pushing," said Roger, getting behind the wheel. Regina

squeezed in alongside him, and because it was still a challenge for her to sit next to a black in the intimate circumstance of a crowded automobile, she motioned Greco to join her and her husband in the front seat, "Because you're the oldest."

Donald and Kenny and Mike crammed themselves into the second seat. Jeb squeezed in with them. Dorry, who had not been fast enough, suffered the humiliation of having to share the rear-facing third seat with Nancy and Bernice, their legs raised over the baskets of food and drink.

"Dad," said Jeb, "can I drive?"

Roger hesitated. He didn't like the idea of turning over a carload of children to a beginning driver. He'd had enough trouble with Harry, who couldn't keep his mind on the road, especially when he borrowed the car for dates. Two moving violations in two years; the second nearly cost Harry a license suspension.

"Please," said Jeb.

He is saying *show me you love me,* Roger thought.

"Oh, let him," said Regina, "he needs the experience. I'm sure he'll be careful."

Roger and Jeb switched places, with Roger squashing in with Donald and Mike and Kenny, and Regina was sandwiched up front, her left leg determined to avoid her son's driving foot, and her right thigh dangerously close to Greco's.

They were off.

Roger seldom had a chance like this to look at the views as they drove, the delicate dogwoods beautiful even after their flowers had dropped, the wild tiger lilies lining the road. He was glad they no longer lived in the city's web. Had life been less tension-filled in previous centuries? *You can't live in another century* is what Regina had said. Yet the youngest member of his committee at the bank, Godwin, had taken up yoga and once, over lunch, had explained how the exercises enabled you to control not just your physical being but also your spirit. Godwin had urged him to try it out, but Roger knew he couldn't just sit doing nothing, even if no one was watching him.

His thoughts meandering, Roger didn't see the stop sign until too late. Jeb must not have seen it at all. He was driving straight past it, Regina yelling, "Stop! Stop!"

The wagon screeched to a halt halfway across the intersection.

"I didn't see it," said Jeb, white-faced.

All three kids in the rearward-facing back seat had turned around, alarm in their faces.

"Lucky there wasn't cross-traffic," said Greco.

"Damn lucky no policeman," said Roger. "You'd have had your first ticket. Weren't you watching?"

"I'm sorry," said Jeb.

Just then they all saw the red Camaro speeding toward the intersection. Jeb threw the car into reverse.

"No!" yelled Roger, swiveling his head. There was a car right behind them, stopped at the stop sign.

Luckily, the Camaro driver spotted them, squealed to a stop. "What the fuck you think you're doing?" yelled the driver.

"Better go forward," said Roger, controlling his voice.

Once safely in the next block, he said, "If you'd backed into that car behind us, the mess of grillwork would have been worth a few hundred dollars in repairs."

"Better that," said Regina, "than getting hit by the Camaro."

"Jeb," said Roger, "want me to take over?"

Regina dreaded Jeb's embarrassment in front of the other kids. She could feel the sweat in her armpits, and the evening was just beginning.

"It's okay, Dad." said Jeb. "I'll be careful."

For the rest of the ride, nobody spoke. All nine passengers were looking about, ready to warn Jeb of any danger.

Just like an airplane ride, Roger thought. *When you get there, it's like another reprieve.*

The sign for Echo Lake Park directed them onto a washboard dirt road, which jounced the heavily loaded wagon. Within seconds, there were dense trees on both sides, and all at once they were in a clearing with room for at least two dozen cars to park, though this evening the place was empty. It was like arriving at a party only to find out it was the wrong night.

"I guess everyone else is watching TV tonight."

"I'm glad we're here," said Regina. Then seeing the children disperse, she yelled, "Hey, don't forget the food! Help get the baskets out the back."

As they returned, she noticed that the back seat was measled with potato-chip flakes.

"Nancy, Bernice, couldn't you wait till we got here?"

"It was Dorry." said Bernice. "He told us to open it."

"That's a lie!" said Dorry.

"That's enough," said Regina. She remembered once reading an article in the *Times Magazine* that said that children were naturally untidy and the ones to worry about were the overly neat children. *Psychiatrists have got everything backward.*

While the kids reluctantly helped Regina unpack the food and place the paper plates and cutlery around the picnic table, Roger went for a short walk along a path softened by years of pine needles. Among the evergreens he saw a single young deciduous tree. The shape of the leaves puzzled him. He grasped a twig at the height of his shoulder and pulled it close enough to study a leaf. Its veins were strangely irregular, like the veins on the back of his own hands.

"Roger?"

He hadn't heard Regina come up behind him.

She took his left hand. His right let the twig snap back. "Come," she said. "Once the aluminum foil is off, the fried eggplant will lose its heat."

And so he ran with her over the springy ground, slowing only just before the picnic table.

The dish of eggplant rounds was empty.

"What happened?" Regina asked at them all. "Did you drop it?"

"We just had one each," said Jeb.

"There are hot dogs and potato salad and cole slaw and what's left of the potato chips and pickles and two apple pies," said Regina in a burst. "Why go and eat the one thing I prepared specially for your father?"

"Never mind," said Roger. "It's all right."

Nancy came up to him, holding something wrapped in foil between her saucered hands. Roger unwrapped the offering. It was a single piece of fried eggplant.

"I saved it for you," Nancy said.

Roger bent to kiss her. "Thank you." He glanced up at the others.

"I didn't know it was anything special," said Greco to Regina.

Jeb knew she thought. *Dorry knew.*

"I derive my satisfaction," said Roger, "from the thought that you made it special."

As he spoke, Roger noticed beside Greco's food-crammed plate a half-pint flask, curved to fit the pocket. "Why that's just like mine," he said, purposefully looking at no one in particular

"I guess they sell a lot of them," said Greco. "I bought it at Walgreen's."

"I wasn't implying that it was mine, just that it looked the same."

"Well, Mr. Maxwell, I wasn't inferring an accusation."

You don't buy flasks like that at Walgreen's, thought Roger, *you buy them at Abercrombie's.* He was sure Greco didn't frequent Abercrombie's. And where did he learn to use words like "inferring"?

"You mind if I ask what's in the flask?"

"Mr. Maxwell, I don't mind you asking anything you like to ask. It's a free country."

"I suppose you'll tell me you carry water in it for emergencies?"

Regina took his arm. The conversation had gone far enough.

"How about soda?" said Greco.

"It would take on the taste of the metal."

"How about watermelon juice?"

It was Donald's snicker that moved Roger to pick up the flask. *The kids knew what was in there.*

"Mind?" said Roger, unscrewing the cap and smelling the whiskey. "Why don't I just hold onto this till later?" he said.

Greco glared as if he had had his civil rights betrayed.

After dinner, the kids went off exploring, with a final caution from Regina to gather back at the car before dark. "Without fail," she said to their retreating backs. "And Nancy, you and Bernice stick with Dorry and his friends. Don't wander off."

"I'm not sure I wouldn't have been better off in the office today," Roger said.

Regina reached across the deserted picnic table for Roger's hand. "It was nice this afternoon," she said.

He didn't answer.

"Wasn't it?"

"Yes," he said.

"Stop thinking about that flask. He's older than the rest."

"I don't think I can contend with drunk kids this evening."

"It's such a tiny flask. I'm sure the others would have had just a nip, if any. If they don't drink in front of you, they'll just drink behind your back. Please, let's go for a walk. I love the lake."

And so they sauntered along the side of the lake, Regina slipping her sandals off and walking in the water, enjoying the liquid cool of it, while Roger stretched out on the bank.

"Hey, Mr. Pensive," she called to him, "why don't you take your shoes and socks off. Just roll your trousers up an inch or two. None of your clients are watching."

He hadn't heard her. Roger's mind had drifted back to his freshman year at Columbia. On his application he had said he wanted to go into law or theology, as had a majority of his male ancestors, but he took advantage of a great teacher, Henry Campbell, to test his assumptions. If his interest was in justice, said Professor Campbell, a career as a lawyer would be inappropriate. And if he pursued theology, he would be a hypocrite as well as poorer than he wanted to be. It was Campbell who pointed out that banking had a dearth of truly educated men, and that with a background in the humanities and social sciences, and later an M.B.A., a young man of his intelligence and sensitivity could go a long way. It was only years later that he realized it was Campbell who had wanted to be a banker and had found a surrogate in a favorite student.

In those early years at the bank, Roger had learned to ferret through a financial statement and pluck out the problems almost instantly, astonishing the client as well as the senior colleague who superintended his work. He learned the phrases that relaxed confrontations with business. *You need money,* he would say; *let's discuss the uses to which it will be put.* He learned how to spot the bad risks quickly: the businessman who always talked about future plans without relation to past and present; the applicant for a line of credit who discreetly bad-mouthed his present bank; the company president who never called to share good news, only bad. Lending money became a sport at which Roger excelled. By the time he was thirty-two, he encountered few opponents who could force him to the net.

Yet he had tired of the peepshow of other people's businesses. Should he strike out on his own as a financial consultant? Still a peepshow. Go into business for himself? Making what, selling it to whom? *You are stuck here for the rest of your life, you've got a litter of responsibilities, you need the money, you can't do anything else well.*

Because his work was so good, the bank indulged him. At Regina's suggestion, he explored the possibility of loans to minority businesses long before it became fashionable or necessary. He reported back—mainly to Regina; his colleagues weren't much interested—that it wasn't a question of lending money; the men he'd met were not part of the business culture (those who were had long ago made out without help), the failure rate would be too high, and charity was a hopeless place to nest his curiosity. He accepted the fact that he was not a saint.

It was Regina, bless her, who had planned that six-week trip to Europe, two days in London, motoring north all the way to Edinburgh and Inverness, then the flight to Amsterdam, Paris, Nice, a car again south to Venice, Florence, a breathless adventure they both loved, but on the flight home from Rome he thought of the bank, and by the time they touched down at Idlewild, the spectacular holiday had come and gone, with nothing changed.

His colleagues at the bank considered him an intellectual,

by which they meant he read books on subjects other than banking. They respected his knowledge of art and consulted him on their purchases, which flattered him and enriched them because good art increased in value faster than securities. In those moments of every business day when a man might seem to be daydreaming or doing nothing, they always assumed Roger was thinking, a compliment to his varied cerebral and artistic interests. Their own were confined to their profession, and golfing or yachting, depending on their income.

Why was he, after all these years, still so restless, still daydreaming of other careers? Halfway through his working life, his command of the business of banking was very nearly complete. All that was left was the politics of high office, the fratricide of successful vice presidents, a sport that for Roger Maxwell held no interest. Through his daily dance of meetings and papers, he saw himself as a man retired while still working, buried in boredom while still alive. Simeon King had thrust railroads across the nation and hunted big game. Was the possibility of adventure the function of the age? What would old Simeon be doing today, his railroads atrophied, the once-virgin landscapes pockmarked by too many people, too much use? *Simeon did what he wanted to do, he didn't care what people thought.* Roger Maxwell was the caretaker of Simeon's house, the zookeeper of his animals.

Stepping out of the water, Regina noticed the expression on Roger's face.

"Hey," she said. "You're miles away. Taking inventory?"

He smiled up at her.

"Include me in," she said, stretching out beside him and putting her head against his shoulder. "Tell me about it."

"Nothing to tell."

"Is it that Cargill person?"

"Maybe."

"Maybe what?"

"You know," he said, "I'm trapped at the bank. The sport's gone."

"But you used to love your work."

"A young man gets a kick out of saying yea or nay to someone who wants money. I'm not a young man. I'm bored with my life."

"With your work."

"Yes."

Was it time for another trip to Europe? she thought, knowing it would be a welcome respite away from the bank and children. Would Bermuda or the Caribbean cure his malaise? Would a love affair with someone else be sufficiently distracting? She was glad of the chance to lie down beside him and cradle his head. In moments, he was dozing.

He liked to poke around plants. If she opened a small nursery with a greenhouse, would Roger enjoy advising her on the business side of things? Business was something he probably needed to get away from. There must be a solution.

When he awoke with a start, Regina realized that she, too, had fallen asleep. The dying sun's red reflection in the lake glowered.

"It's almost dark," she said. "What time is it?"

"Eight o'clock," said Roger, scrambling to his feet. They checked the area around the picnic table, then the car. No one.

"Good thing I keep a flashlight in the car," he said.

Armed with it, they went off in search of the renegades.

They thought they heard children's voices several times and called out "Hellooo!" in vain.

"Do you suppose they hear us?" Regina asked.

He prodded the darkness ahead of their steps with the weak beam of the flashlight, saw that the path through the woods forked

"Try the left one," she said.

"Do you hear them?"

"Just intuition."

The left fork went slightly downhill. Then the woods broke. They were at the lake, shimmering now in moonlight.

"Hellooo," shouted Roger.

"I'll bet they're following us and enjoying it," she said.

"This isn't a joke."

They retraced their steps uphill from the water, finding the fork, and taking the right one this time.

"Wait," said Regina, halting him.

They both heard the sound of a girl crying.

"It doesn't sound like Nancy," she said. "Could be Bernice."

They were trotting now.

"Watch out for low branches," said Roger. "You could get the point of one right in the eye."

The pine needles that had felt so good underfoot earlier now seemed a slippery menace as they homed in on the sound.

Suddenly it stopped, like a phonograph arm being lifted. At that moment, they both saw the small, strangely lit clearing to the right.

The light came from three candles stuck on the bottom of tin cans. Where had they come from? Who had prepared for this?

All eight were there. Jeb had his hand over Bernice's mouth. That's why her crying had stopped so suddenly. Roger poked his flashlight's beam. The kids were in a semicircle near a tree. From a low limb, something swayed.

"Oh my God," said Regina.

A thrashing squirrel with a cord around its neck was hanging from the limb.

"Cut that down!" Roger ordered.

Jeb took his hand away from Bernice's mouth. She was only whimpering now that Roger and Regina had arrived.

"It's still alive!" said Regina.

"Take that down," Roger repeated.

Jeb started to untie the knot around the tree. The squirrel was now barely twitching.

"Hurry!"

Greco flicked open a switchblade and with one short motion cut the cord. The squirrel, the cord still around its neck, shuddered on the ground.

Roger knelt, put the flashlight down so that its beam was on the squirrel, and tried to untie the cord.

"Don't let it bite you," said Greco, "you could get rabies from it."

This animal couldn't bite anyone. It's nearly dead, Roger thought, as at last it was free of the cord around its neck.

"Daddy, why doesn't it run away?" asked Nancy.

Their eyes were riveted on the pathetic animal.

"I think it had better be put out of its misery," said Roger quietly.

Greco changed the position of the switchblade in his hand. As he knelt to stab the squirrel, Regina said, "No, no, please not that!"

The blade stopped in mid-air. Jeb took two steps forward and stomped on the animal's head. Regina could hear the bones crunch.

The head was pulped.

Looking straight at the kneeling boy with the knife, Roger said "Whose idea was this?"

Greco pointed the knife at Jeb.

"Jeb," said Regina, "what got into you all? Why . . ." Her unfinished question hung helplessly in the air.

Jeb said, "We wanted to cut the fur off the tail. We wanted to see if under the fur the tail was like a rat."

"Why in front of the little girls?" Regina pleaded.

"They wanted to watch," said Jeb. "Then Bernice chickened out."

"But why did you *hang* it?" her heart cried.

It was Dorry who answered. "For the fun of it."

Roger looked at the circle of faces. *Maybe I'm not fit to be a father*, he thought.

5

REGINA AND ROGER lay stretched in bed, immobilized by exhaustion. Only the dim light of the alarm clock glowed in the dark.

Finally, she said, "Let's not talk about it any more. Let's try to get a night's sleep."

Roger reached over to his night table for the small plastic box that contained the soft earplugs that would shut out the sound of the leaves in the wind outside, the clock ticking, Regina's breathing, everything except the noises inside his own head. His earplug habit was the shutting of a cell door against the rest of the world.

Just as he was putting the first plug into his right ear, the sound of gravel thrown up by a car in the driveway made him sit bolt upright. "What's that?"

Regina was already out of bed and looking. "Greco's car, it's leaving."

"Good riddance."

"I do wish you'd been nicer to that boy."

"Nineteen is no boy."

A cricket mocked his voice.

"Besides," he continued, "I don't see why I should make amends for your Southern childhood. I treat him the same way I'd treat anyone his age who acts the way he does."

"That may not be good enough. They've got catching up to do, hear?" She turned and saw that he had stuffed his earplugs back in his ears. He had not heard.

Roger, his eyes closed, the first day of his weekend fled, felt his bones ache with tiredness. Was escape the only way to rest, go off somewhere without the children? Whatever you do, however much you care, it all turned into a holding operation, keeping the peace until they left you, drained. Was he wrong in wondering why Jeb chose Greco as a friend? Three years was a marked difference at that age. In his day, sixteens didn't consort with nineteens unless they purposely latched onto troublemakers. Was Jeb trying to say *we don't pay attention any more to things like age and color the way you and Mom do?* Jeb couldn't be oblivious to what his mother and father saw. His friends were extremes: the Donald boy so passive, doing everything Jeb wanted him to do, that Greco looking for a fight. Why not other boys like Jeb, the sane middle, like his own friends?

When he had been Jeb's age, he had had close friends. All Hackley students, all with parents who could afford boarding school. But how that changed when he went to Columbia! There, his closest friends were Fred, a book-hungry Jew, obsessively wanting to know everything; Larry, who was Greek or Armenian and who wanted to be the architect of cities, not buildings. Only Chet was a Wasp like himself. They were all so close, even the girls from Barnard—what did Chet call them, the Mediterranean rabble trying to pass as Americans? God, that time they all drove to New Jersey with the girls, nine of them packed into the rattletrap that was missing its right front door? Good thing the police hadn't stopped them! All that beer, the dark girl who had come with someone else ending with him, then learning her name was a nickname and that her real name was Sonia, and he, beery, had said what kind of name was that? Her eyes blazed as she told him her parents were from Russia, she assured him they had accents, and wouldn't let him past the threshold because he was a certified *goy*. She had said Wasps were a guilt-stricken minority, hoping their exotic friends wouldn't think their interest in the arts was any the less because generations of inbreeding had drained all Gentiles of passion and curiosity. Sonia said the Jukes were Wasps, the Kalikaks were Wasps, and what Roger needed was to fuck an Eskimo, and he had countered that the Eskimos were more inbred than the Wasps. It wasn't all joking; the girl Chet had married—what was her name, Esther?—it couldn't have been more Old Testament. He remembered his father saying "What strange friends you have?" when he brought some of them home one weekend, and his answer, "What strange friends you have, Dad—they're all the same!" Those days were great for him; it was like opening up windows all over a big new house, each new vista a surprise.

All sorts of new directions excited him, and even after he had decided not to pursue the occupations of his forebears, the law or the ministry, he thought the atmosphere of his diverse companions made it forever impossible for him to get lost in one of those latter-day monasteries, the Rockefeller Foundation or the Ford Foundation, places it was proper for someone with his background to hide in uselessly for the rest of his life, handing out money to safe artists and to scientists who knew when not to step out of line. How had banking been different? Unlike the foundations, it had to show a profit. His kind of banking—if fellows like Cargill could be kept in line—was safer than the foundations. You got your money back. Good times or bad times, you could ask a price that guaranteed a profit. Men like himself could go through a lifetime without ever making a bad loan. Where were the risks? Would any of his venturesome friends in the crammed rattletrap have gone into banking? *Not on your life*. Where had they gone to?

Time, wives, jobs had flung them their separate ways. Why had he not made a greater effort to keep in touch? At least with one of them?

Which one?

Anyone.

If your son's friends are not like your son, that is a virtue; your friends now are all like you.

If Regina took the kids for a drive tomorrow and they got hit by a trailer truck, whom would you turn to, friendless Roger, what person? Your friends were your equals, weren't they? Have you encapsulated yourself within your family because that is the one place that you indisputably govern. Govern? Harry's gone off, next'll be Jeb. Why the squirrel-hanging, though? Environment? Heredity? He was responsible for both. Harry hadn't done things like . . . or wasn't he remembering?

He remembered Harry and Regina's cat. Harry'd been teasing the cat with a string as if it were a kitten, and the cat had swiped at the dangling cord, scratching Harry's wrist deep enough to open a vein. The doctor had suggested a tetanus shot because it was an outdoor cat that wandered who knows where.

When the cat disappeared, Regina was inconsolable. They roamed the nearby streets and woods for two days. On the third day, Regina had given up on its return.

On the fourth day, Roger investigated a sound he heard from the attic as he passed near the trap door. He lowered the attic stairs, climbed them with trepidation, and pulled the string that lit the naked bulb dangling from the attic ceiling. The moment he saw the cardboard shoe box tied with the same cord Harry had used to tease the cat with and whiffed the smell exuding from the box, he knew what was inside. It had to be alive, from the sounds it was making. He carried the moving box downstairs and around to the back of the house near the garden hose, knowing the cat had fouled itself, against all the rules of catdom. He hoped to be able to hose it down before Regina saw it. But the moment he cut the cord, the cat bounded from the box and ran off into the woods, this time never to return. He had kept the secret from Regina, who privately called her son Sweet Harry. Roger did not want Regina, who thought of Huck Finn as a terrible boy, to think of Harry as a monster.

Job's first curse was a houseful of children!

But then, before long their house would no longer be the habitat of children. A few years and Dorry would be off to school, then Nancy in—what?—less than ten, and Regina and he would be together alone, back to the childless beginning. Was parenthood worth all that frantic care only to be deserted in the end? Did it make sense?

Making love in the afternoon had made sense. With the kids gone they could do what they liked when they liked. He glanced over in Regina's direction. She was not asleep. Up on one elbow, she was listening to what? Roger pulled one earplug out.

"I don't hear anything," he said.

"Greco's car came back."

"Shit." The second he said it, he was sorry. He hated to use words like that, it was so undisciplined.

"You didn't give him his flask back. He probably went for some liquor."

"Nothing's open this time of night. If he needed some that badly, he could have stolen some of ours downstairs."

"He's your son's guest. If a guest helps himself to food or liquor in your house, he is not stealing." She had the top sheet pulled up to her chin.

"I'm sorry. I'm very tired. Let's not fight."

"Put your earplug back in and go to sleep."

Regina's hand on his shoulder was shaking him awake. Roger glanced at the clock: 1:00 A.M. He'd barely been asleep.

She motioned him to take the plugs out of his ears.

"Listen."

He heard the sounds of water splashing. For a moment he thought a pipe had burst. Then the cries of several voices focused his attention on the out-of-doors.

Roger struggled out of bed, put his numbed feet into his slippers, and went out on the balcony. In the bright moonlight below, he could see, perhaps thirty yards from the house, the waves in the swimming pool overflowing the edges. What was going on at this hour of the night? At that instant a nude body ran into view. It must have been one of the older ones. He could see the dark pubic hair, but, strangely, no penis swung beneath the dark triangle.

"They're skinny-dipping," he said, putting his bathrobe on.

"Oh well," said Regina, "I said they could have their friends for the weekend and I guess this is all part of it."

Goddamn it, it's my weekend, too, Roger thought.

Regina recognized the wrath in his face. *They're only children,* she thought.

"I'll come with you," she said.

They both walked carefully in order not to trip.

"The noise at the pool," said Roger, "is loud enough for Akin to hear down below. That bastard'll call the police."

"Oh, I'm sure he wouldn't."

"He hates kids."

"They don't have experience with children, that's all."

"Lucky bastard."

"Roger!"

They were close enough to the pool now to hear one of the voices very clearly yelling "Stop! Stop!"

Roger found the lamppost at the head of the stairs leading to the pool area. He flicked the switch, flooding the place with light.

"Turn the fucking light out!" a boy's voice yelled.

"It's your father, man!"

The voice that had cried "Stop!" was now yelling "Let me go!"

Roger, his hand shading his eyes, saw Greco at the far side of the pool, his black cock hanging. He was holding a pole across the pool. Jeb, naked, was holding the other end. Tied to the center of the pole was a kitchen chair, and strapped in the chair, his hands and feet tied, was Donald, yelling to be let go.

"Hey, Dad," said Jeb, his speech slurred, "turn the light out! Mom, make him turn the light out!"

"What the hell are you doing?" Roger bellowed.

"We're having fun! Ducking chair. Donald lost."

"Lost what?"

"The game. He gets ducked three times."

"Why are you all naked?" asked Regina.

"We were born that way!" Greco called.

"Get that boy out of that chair this instant," said Roger.

Greco and Jeb walked the pole—it must have been heavy with its load—to the end of the pool, setting Donald down.

It was only then that Roger saw at the corner of the pool the naked form he had spied fleetingly from the balcony. It wasn't a boy. It was Matilda.

"What is she doing here?" he whispered to Regina. "How did she get here?"

But Regina, who had heard him, did not answer. She was

hurrying over to the outdoor bar at the other end of the pool. Sitting on bar stools, Roger could now see, were Dorry, Kenny, and Mike. They at least had their pajamas on, though the pajamas were soaking wet. Had they been swimming in them, or had they put them on soaking wet?

Regina singled out Dorry. "You've been drinking!"

Dorry opened his mouth, but said nothing. Kenny slipped from the stool, walked toward Regina, fell to his knees. "Hoosh drinking?" he said.

"Regina! Come here!" It was Roger. She hurried to him, looking back once at Dorry and Mike trying to lift Kenny up between them.

Roger was standing over where the huge old rhododendrons ran along the south side of the pool area. Nancy and Bernice, both naked, were hugging each other in misery.

"Why did you take your clothes off?" asked Regina.

Nancy looked like she was going to be sick. "They said."

"They said what."

"We had to, just like Matilda, or we couldn't stay up like the big ones."

"You both get up to the house, right now. Do you have a towel?"

"We weren't swimming."

"Get going now."

Jeb and Greco had untied Donald.

"Get that chair back up to the kitchen," said Roger.

Matilda wrapped one of their Yves Saint Laurent bath towels around herself avoiding their eyes.

It was then that Roger found, in clear view at the poolside, where all glass was prohibited, three bottles emptied of his best champagne. He felt his hands shake.

"Why don't you drink your own junk?" he said to Jeb. "That vintage is expensive and irreplaceable. Get dressed, you hear me, all of you!" He walked toward Matilda now that she had covered herself. "How did you get here? Where are your clothes?"

"Upstairs," said Matilda.

"How'd you get here?"

The girl gestured at Greco.

"Well, you take her right on home," Roger said to Greco.

"I can't go home," said Matilda, shivering in her towel. "My parents are away for the weekend."

"Where'd he pick you up?"

"His house."

"You were staying at his house?" Roger shot a glance at Regina. "Maybe you should both go there right now."

Jeb, weaving slightly, walked close enough to say, "They're my friends. You said I could have my friends over."

"Let them go to bed," said Regina. "Party's over for the night."

The kids straggled toward the house, each wrapped in whatever towel he had brought down to the pool, except Greco, who carried his towel over his left arm, and with his right led Matilda by the elbow.

Roger whispered to Regina, "Look at him, naked. What do we do about her?"

"In a guest bedroom, I suppose."

"What's to keep him from coming down to her room?"

"What's to keep any of them?" said Regina, resigned. Just then she saw that Nancy and Bernice had stopped short of the house, and were huddled over the grass. There was an unmistakable sound. Both of them were throwing up.

Regina got Nancy and Bernice settled in one of the nearer second-floor bedrooms, where they could get to her more easily if they needed help during the night. Then she checked on the three twelve-year-olds. Mike and Dorry were sitting on Kenny's bed. Kenny looked miserable.

"You two get into your beds," she said. "Don't let Kenny

drink water or anything when he gets up in the morning."

She wasn't sure it had registered. She switched off their light and closed the door, made her way to her own bedroom, where Roger, lying in bed, was staring at the ceiling.

She looked to see if he had his earplugs in. They were in his hand.

Regina went to his side of the bed, sat, put a hand to his brow. "It'll be better tomorrow."

"It's been tomorrow for a couple of hours already," said Roger.

SATURDAY

6

WHEN ROGER AWOKE alone in bed it was past nine o'clock, later than he had slept for years.

Through the window he could see the leaves on the trees buffeted by the west wind. A complaisant parent was like a tree, acted upon, not acting.

Was Regina fixing breakfast? The kids, on weekends, were inclined to sleep half the day away. Perhaps she was preparing breakfast just for the two of them. That would be nice.

He heard the chipmunk scurrying. Two houses ago their bedroom had been under the attic, and an occasional squirrel or chipmunk had got in after the rain. If you didn't do anything about it, scurrying feet could wake you during the night. Fortunately, the squirrel repellent he bought could be scattered like mothballs in the attic, and the smell would keep the rodents out of there for months. But the one he heard now had somehow gotten in between the second and third floors. You wouldn't want to break a hole in the bedroom ceiling or in the floor of the Bestiary. Perhaps he ought to let the exterminator worry about this one.

It was the word "exterminator" that brought back the memory of the squirrel hanging from the tree.

Just then the bedroom door swung open, pushed by Regina's toe, and in she came in her lavender robe carrying a tray with a tall glass of orange juice, coffee, and a plate with two fried eggs over, crisp bacon, and a cloth napkin rolled in a ring. It had been years since she had done that.

"Looks great!" he said, out of bed in an instant.

"Get back in. This is supposed to be breakfast in bed."

"Just brush teeth, that's all," said Roger.

In less than a minute he was back in bed, and Regina moved the tray from the foot of the bed to his lap.

"Where's yours?" he asked.

"I'm bringing it now. I forgot to push the lever when I put the bread in the toaster."

She was gone in a swirl of lavender.

"Remember that weekend in Atlantic City," she said when she returned, setting down the tray, taking off her robe, and slipping into bed beside him. "That waiter who brought us breakfast in bed said we couldn't possibly be Mr. and Mrs. since we were huddled on the one side of the big bed?"

"He probably says something like that to everyone. You know . . ."

She could tell he was no longer in Atlantic City. "Yes?"

"Last night, first the squirrel, then the swimming pool. When we came home from Atlantic City, remember. the nursemaid said what an angel Harry was?"

"They're all angels at six months!"

In the distance, they both heard the front doorbell ring.

"Newspaper?"

"I brought it in," said Regina.

"I'll go," said Roger, wiping his lips. "I'm almost done."

He put the tray aside, slipped into his bathrobe and brushed his hand through his hair.

Going down the stairs, he wondered who it could be at nine-thirty on a Saturday morning. Much too early for the cleaner's delivery truck.

"Who is it?" he said through the door.

"Tim Ryan." It was not the voice of a man. He didn't know any Tim Ryan.

Roger opened the door. It was two steps down to the gravel driveway. Standing there was a boy about Jeb's age, maybe a year older. The nervous boy reminded him of the applicants at his desk in the days when he ruled on personal loans, the sort of person who looked as if he had already been to several other banks first, not knowing they all checked with a central credit agency.

"Greco here?" asked the boy. "I was at his place. They said he was here."

"He's probably still asleep. The kids were all up late last night."

Roger noticed the boy's bicycle for the first time. It was a long haul by bicycle from Greco's side of the tracks.

"I'll see if he's awake," said Roger. Regina would be eating her breakfast in bed alone. His coffee would be getting cold.

"Come in," he said to the boy. "Wait here."

Roger climbed the two flights to the Bestiary Room. He turned the knob. The door barely budged.

He tried again, then heard the sound of bare feet, then of an object being moved away from the door. Jeb opened it, bleary-eyed from sleep.

"What'd you put a chair under the doorknob for?" asked Roger.

"Privacy. You didn't knock."

"I didn't want to wake everybody up."

"You woke me up."

"Someone's at the door for Greco. Tim Ryan."

"What's he doing here?"

"You know him?"

"Sure. From school."

"He wants to see Greco."

"Greco isn't here," said Jeb.

From the doorway, Roger quickly glanced around the room.

"I said he wasn't here, Dad."

"Where is he?"

"I'll get him." Jeb went down to the second floor. Roger followed.

"I said I'd get him."

Roger waited as Jeb, without knocking, opened the door of the bedroom Matilda had been given. There were whispers.

Jeb came out. "He's coming." Roger watched Jeb trudge upstairs.

Greco took his time coming out. He was wearing only undershorts, the rest of him an expanse of black skin topped by frizzy hair that had not been combed. Instinctively, Roger brushed his hand over his own uncombed hair.

"He's downstairs, at the front door." said Roger.

"Thanks."

Roger moved a few steps down the hall toward his bedroom, then retraced his steps to the stairwell. He could hear the voices, Greco's hushed, the Ryan boy's anxious.

"What the hell you doin chasing me down here?"

"I tried to get you yesterday."

"I'm out any time I want to be out. What you want? I don't do retail no more, you know that."

Roger observed the unformed sentences.

"I'm taking two girls up to my father's place in New Hampshire."

"One for him?"

"He's on a business trip."

"What a kid like you need two girls for? How much you need?"

'Two dimes' worth?"

"You asking or telling?"

"I told them I'd get some, that's why they're coming. The guy they get grass from moved to Canada."

"Moved or ran?"

"How should I know, Grec. Please, this is real important. These two chicks are a combo. They're terrific. I just gotta have the grass."

"All I got is super one A. Two dimes'll cost you thirty."

"Can't do thirty, Grec. I need something for gas and beer."

"That your problem, boy."

"Please, Grec."

"How about one dime for fifteen?"

"I told them two. The deal is, what we don't use, they get to take back."

"I don't want to spoil your combo, kid. When can you pay the rest?"

"Next week?"

"Next week you pay ten plus five interest."

"Jesus, Grec, that makes thirty-five for two dimes!"

"Why don't you go on home."

"Okay."

"Gimme your twenty, man. I'm not standing around here in my underwear for fun."

Tim gave Greco two folded bills.

"You wait here," said Greco.

Roger quickly turned the corner of the hallway, went into his bedroom, listened at the ceiling for Greco's footsteps.

"What's the matter?" asked Regina. "Who is it?"

Roger held a finger to his lips. He had left the bedroom door open. "Be right back."

In the hallway, he could hear Greco coming back down the stairs. Roger inched close to the stairwell, but dared not get as close as he had been before. He heard the voices but not the words of the transaction taking place down below.

Back in his bedroom, he closed the door.

"That boy—" he said to Regina.

"Which?"

"Greco. He's selling pot. He's brought it into this house."

He lifted the cup of coffee to his lips. It was tepid.

He was lost in thought when Regina said, "Do you think Jeb and Donald are into—"

"You realize," he said to her, "that under the law, we're responsible if there's stuff in this house? I should call the police."

Regina slid out of bed. "I wouldn't like to explain to a policeman. We've got a houseful of children."

"I'll handle it."

"Why don't you wait till everybody's up. You can have a word with Jeb. Maybe together we can find some suitable reason for sending Greco home."

"And Matilda."

"What's she got to do with it?"

"He spent the night in her bedroom."

Regina watched his face.

"What I can't figure out," he said, "is why Greco went to the Bestiary Room."

"Roger?"

"Yes."

"Perhaps you're jumping to conclusions. Couldn't it be something innocent?"

"I think the innocents in this house are you and me."

REGINA CAME up behind Roger as he was slapping aftershave on his cheeks.

"I want that Greco and his junk out of this place."

"Let it pass till Sunday. They're all leaving then. Talk to Jeb afterward. If he sees how you feel, he won't invite Greco back."

"He'll do as he wants. That kid is not in our control."

"Roger, it's we who have to stay in control. Sixteen is a difficult age."

"You've said that at every age he's been. My best champagne, pffft!"

Regina watched him in the mirror. "I'm sorry about the champagne, but agonizing about it won't make it come back. Let's not spoil today because of what happened yesterday." She put her hands on the muscles between his neck and shoulders and kneaded them gently. "Hurt?"

"No."

"It's our weekend off, too. You always enjoy a drive. Please let's go."

"We can't leave the little ones in the house with that bunch. They torture each other, not just squirrels."

"Oh, Roger, you're getting paranoid."

He turned to face her.

"I'm sorry," she said quickly. "When Nancy and Bernice wake up, all they'll have energy for is commiserating over their first hangovers together."

"Kids that age drinking!"

"Didn't you ever do anything like that when you were nine?"

"Drink? Never."

"I wasn't perfect. I'm sure you weren't. Are you coming?"

"I remember . . ."

"Remember what?" asked Regina.

"When kids tried to emulate their parents."

"Oh, I'm not so sure we're always models of perfect behavior."

"I don't get falling down drunk."

She remembered when he had and the children had all seen. "I don't think they're ready for A.A. just yet. Let them sleep it off. They depend on the kindness of strangers."

"Parents are not strangers."

"Are you so sure?"

Roger was no longer sure.

"I'm going," she said. "I do hope you're coming along, sir."

Roger wished the Buick he was guiding down the gravel driveway were a convertible. With a windy day in the offing, it'd be nice on a country road, like being in a power boat on the Hudson opened up all the way.

The car windows open, accelerating when the road was clear, he knew the pleasure the kids talked about when they said they wanted wheels. More like wings. Jeb talked of wandering in Europe for a year after high school. This new generation just gets up and goes. He envied them their mobility, their sexual ease, their seeming carelessness.

Regina glanced at the side of Roger's face tensed over the wheel.

"What are you thinking?" she asked.

"Guess."

"It's great to be away from the house."

"No."

"It's good getting away from the kids."

"No."

"Tell me."

"One of my reckless fantasies."

"Maybe I'd better not hear."

"If the front axle broke right now and I lost control, we'd hit that stone wall and—" he glanced at her—"the kids would have one hundred seventy thousand dollars of insurance, take over the house, have their friends in for a permanent party."

"Why don't we wait a while on that?"

Roger smiled. "Actually, I was thinking about a power boat. As a change. As a thing to get out of the house to."

"We've had the expense of the new house . . ."

"It was just an idea. We wouldn't use the boat all that much. Funny, you long for something, then when you finally buy it, you use it at first. then less and less."

Regina thought it was true of people, also. She had been dating Harley exclusively when she met Roger. Harley had hung on at first. When the outcome was clear, he had vanished. But then, after she had been married for a year, one morning Harley had called her.

Old Roger still paying enough attention to you? he had said.

The truth was that Roger, who had consumed her in the months after her marriage, had turned to each new opportunity at the bank like an adolescent boy on a heart-stopping date with a new girl, unsure of himself, nervously investigating, then bold and assertive, talking to her about his conquests at the bank in terms that reminded Regina of their courtship.

"You're a wicked man," she had said lightly to Harley.

"If you're feeling wicked, too . . ." Harley had said, but she had stopped him.

"Harley, I remember an expression of yours. Wick-dipping is one thing, love is another. I think you've got some learning to do."

On their first anniversary, Roger had said they were going out, but he wouldn't name a show or a restaurant. She got dressed up—she remembered how he looked her up and down when he came home from the office—and he took her in the car driving down country roads till, deep in the woods, he found a dead end, parked, and made love to her in the back seat. Afterward, they laughed like kids at how they had messed their clothes and tortured their bodies only to kiss, and kiss again, and then, like acrobats, once more joined in inadequate space, they overwhelmed their expectations, Regina saying *We have a bedroom, you know* and Roger saying things like *I can't bring the car up into the bedroom* and *How'd you like to do it in the bank* and she said *Where in the bank* and he said *In the vault, in the Directors' room, on my desk, take your pick*, and they had laughed themselves silly. Of course they had taken no precautions, and she had sometimes been tempted to tell their eldest, Harry, that he had been conceived in the back of a car.

Roger interrupted her reverie. "I guess," he was saying, "we should find out what the kids are up to in case you need to do something."

"Like what?" said Regina, puzzled.

"Talk to Dr. Keeler about last night."

"He's not a psychiatrist," said Regina.

"You said he seems to understand children."

"I'm not thinking about the children. I'm thinking . . ." She glanced at him. "Of the back seat of this car."

Roger looked at her. He knew what she was remembering. "It's broad daylight," he said.

"I won't tell my husband."

He laughed.

She had accomplished her mission. She had gotten his mind off his problems. "Drive," she said, as he stepped on the accelerator.

By the time they started back, Saturday traffic had built up. They arrived home after eleven. The kitchen looked as if dozens of people had eaten there, leaving half-filled cereal dishes, eggshells on the counter, dried eggs on plates, coffee cups with cigarettes put out in the bottom, milk not put away, a trail of sugar two feet long crunching underfoot. The locust children had come and gone.

Regina immediately set herself to putting the dishes on the dishwasher counter, gathering balled-up paper napkins.

"You ought to make them pick up after themselves."

"Oh," she said, "you know they won't."

"If we dropped dead today, they'd have to pick up after themselves."

She followed his gaze to the plate she was reaching for.

"Don't pick that up!"

The center of the plate was a sticky glop, the remains of pancakes and syrup. Roger picked a small piece of twisted paper from the edge, held it to his nose.

"What is it?" she said.

"What does it look like to you?"

She hesitated. "The butt end of a homemade cigarette?"

Roger was out of the room before her question was finished. He bounded up the stairs. From the Bestiary Room came the throb of amplified music. He threw the door open, motioned for Jeb to step out.

Jeb closed the door behind him.

"What's up, Dad?"

Roger held the twisted butt in front of Jeb's nose. "Who was using this?"

"Hey, Dad, you're hurting my arm."

Roger hadn't realized he'd gripped the boy. He let go.

"Who?" he demanded.

"I guess it wasn't Harry. He isn't here," said Jeb.

"Don't play smart-ass with me. Who?"

Jeb moved farther down the hall, away from the Bestiary Room door. Inside, the music had stopped.

Roger said, "It wasn't Bernice or Nancy, right?"

"I guess."

"Or Dorry and his friends."

"I wouldn't know. I wasn't watching everybody. I'm not a cop."

"Was it you?"

"I don't use that stuff, Dad."

"Then it can only be Donald." Roger hesitated purposefully. "Or that Greco boy."

Jeb was silent.

"Get him," Roger ordered.

Jeb went into the Bestiary, closing the door behind him. Roger could hear voices. Then Greco came out, hitching his pants the way cowboys do in the movies.

"You wanted to talk to me, Mr. Maxwell?"

"This yours?" He held the twisted butt end up.

"Well," said Greco, his face spread in a smile, "it used to be."

"What does that mean?"

"I gave it to Jeb as a kind of hospitality present, you know? He shouldn'a left it. He shoulda flushed it like I said."

Roger swung open the Bestiary Room door. The five boys were huddled in one corner of the room. "Come here, Jeb."

Jeb stepped out into the hallway.

"You said you didn't use it," Roger said.

Jeb said to Greco, "You told."

"Now listen here, man, you just told your old man it was me, didn't you? Some of you white mothers got the brains of a baby. I told you that whatever didn't go up in smoke went down the toilet."

Roger spoke to his son. "You bought this from him?"

"He didn't buy nothing from nobody. I gave it to him."

Roger felt a warning pulse in his temples.

Softly, Roger said to Greco, "I think you better leave."

"That's nice, real nice. He gets caught and I get to leave."

"I don't want things like that brought into the house. I don't want you in this house again."

"Now, Mr. Maxwell, aren't you being a bit hysterical bout nothing?"

"I heard you sell some to that young boy this morning. I should have told you to get out then."

"Mr. Maxwell, that boy Tim needed some grass and he was going to get some somewhere cause he had a party going. If he didn't get it from me, he'd get some off of somewhere. He always do. I'm just supplying a service, same as any business-man. Don't you sell money at your bank?"

"You'd better take your things and leave."

"Okay. Just cool it." Greco strode into the Bestiary.

"You mothers all get the hell out of this room for now."

Dorry and his friends scrambled out the door, glancing at Mr. Maxwell as they went. Then Donald, at a nod from Greco, left also.

"I'm getting my things," said Greco.

Roger stood still.

"You gonna stand there and watch? You think I'm gonna

steal something of yours? I don't need nothing of yours." He came closer to Roger. "You got something of mine."

Roger looked puzzled.

"My flask."

Roger went down to the bedroom, got the flask, quickly came back up the stairs to the Bestiary. As he walked in the door, he saw Greco in back of the brown bear.

"Here." He held out the flask.

Greco couldn't take it from him because his arms were full, holding a kilo-sized package of grass. Roger took three or four steps so that he could see behind the bear.

The stuffed bear's back was folded open.

"Sorry to lose one helluva good hiding place, Mr. Maxwell. Why don't you just stuff that flask in my pocket. My hands are kinda full."

Roger threw the flask in the direction of the nearest bunk bed. It missed, hit a post, fell to the floor. They both heard the inside glass break.

"Son of a bitch," said Greco.

"What did you say?"

"You heard me. I paid good money for that flask."

Roger turned and briskly walked from the room.

"Hey, where you going?"

Roger could hear Greco following him. He headed for his bedroom on the second floor.

Greco caught up to him at the bedroom door. "I said what you doing?"

Roger tried to shut the door so he could lock it. Greco put a foot out.

"What is it, Roger?" Regina came out of the bathroom into their bedroom.

Greco, holding the kilo with both hands, pushed the door open farther with his knee.

"This is our bedroom," said Roger. "Get your foot away."

"I want to know what you doing."

At the door, Roger said to Regina, "Call 901-2100. Tell them to send a squad car quickly."

With a heave, Greco lunged at the door. Roger staggered backward. Greco put the kilo down, then went for Regina at the phone. She was dialing as Greco grabbed the instrument out of her hands and with one tremendous yank ripped it from its mooring in the wall.

"Don't you put no cops on me! I can prove you've stashed that grass in your house for months, that you're dealing it and using me!"

Greco grabbed his kilo and ran downstairs.

Roger followed him out of the house. Greco opened the trunk of his car, threw the kilo in, came back to the back door, which Roger stood blocking. Regina behind him.

"Out of my way," said Greco.

Roger felt eyes watching out of windows. Were the children witnessing all this?

"This is my house," said Roger, feeling a sudden rush of guilt. Could this boy, however rich he became from dealing dope, ever own or live in a house like this?

"I've got to get my things," Greco persisted.

"You got your things."

Just then Matilda appeared behind Regina, said "Excuse me," and went past both Maxwells. "What's going on?" she asked Greco.

"Just get in the car and shut up," he ordered her. Then to Maxwell, "Out of my way. I have some stuff downstairs."

"Downstairs where?"

"The basement."

"Where in the basement?"

"Just get out of my way, mother." In one motion, Greco

whipped out the switchblade he had wanted to stab the squirrel with the night before. With his left hand, he threw his car keys at Matilda. "Start the engine," he ordered her.

"Let him past," Regina whispered.

Roger made room for Greco to get by.

Once inside, Greco headed for the cellar stairs, Roger following. "Get my flashlight," he told Regina, who went to the pantry for the five-celled light.

As soon as Greco was inside the boiler room, Roger slammed the door shut tight, hoping the warped wood jammed.

"Hey, man, what's going on?" Greco shouted from inside.

Roger braced his back against the door, knees bent, but there was nothing within reach to give him leverage. He flicked the switch outside the boiler-room door.

"What the fuck you doing? How'm I supposed to find something in the dark?"

Roger heard footsteps inside, then felt the first lunge against the door. He'd never be able to hold it.

Regina appeared at the top of the cellar stairs, holding the flashlight. He waved at her to come down. She handed him the long flashlight just as Greco lunged against the door a second time.

"I gonna kill you, you son of a bitch."

He couldn't hold the door much longer. Regina saw the line of sweat drops across Roger's forehead.

"Please," he said, "call the police right now from the kitchen phone. Or get my gun."

"I'll call," she said, going up the stairs.

"Hurry!"

Roger held his back as hard as he could against the boiler-room door. Then the third lunge came. It seemed for a second as if his spine would shatter. Quickly, he moved away from the door, turned the flashlight on, held it straight at head height, hoping the light would blind Greco as he burst the door open from the dark room.

Greco's next lunge received resistance only from the jamb; the door flew open, nearly sent him sprawling. He threw an arm up to shield his eyes from the light. Roger saw that Greco still held the open knife. *Hurry, Regina!* He had to somehow stall for time.

"I'll hold the light," he said, "so you can find what you're looking for."

"Turn the overhead on," Greco commanded.

Roger obeyed, flicked the switch on.

Greco turned, darted for the far side of the boiler room. He was squeezing himself behind the boiler.

Roger stepped into the room to see.

Greco cursed. Had he hurt himself?

When he squeezed out from behind the boiler, he had a second kilo in his hand.

"Now get out of my way," he said to Roger, standing in front of the open doorway.

Roger didn't move. *Don't be a fool,* he told himself.

Greco pointed the knife at Roger's face. "I could buy and sell you, Mr. Banker," Greco said. "I gotta git some up on the second floor."

"What?"

"Out of my way." Greco swished the knife. "Or I'll leave you with a souvenir."

Roger stepped out of the way.

"You monkey with me now and I'll be back for Nancy."

Greco went for the basement door. Roger stepped after him. "You what?"

Greco swirled. "You heard me, you white motherfucker."

Both hands on the foot-long flashlight, Roger swung at the pointing blade, smashing it from Greco's hand.

"Son of a bitch," said Greco in surprise as the knife clattered on the concrete floor. Roger moved to step on it. Greco got there first, stooped to pick it up, and Roger, feeling old for violence, not knowing how to defend himself against the expected slashes of the knife, summoned his strength and smashed his flashlight down at the stooping boy's head with force and rage.

Something in Greco's head gave.

Without screaming, the stooped boy dropped the kilo, fell in slow motion, dark blood bubbling from his head and ears.

On the floor, Greco seemed an oversized black doll, its limbs askew.

My God, thought Roger, the flashlight trembling in his hand. He backed up, then turned, careful to avoid tripping over the step at the door.

He slammed the basement door shut behind him, held onto the banister, forced himself to climb the stairs to the kitchen.

Regina, phone in hand, turned in fear, saw it was Roger. "Thank heaven. I misdialed twice. I got the wrong number. Help me."

Roger took the receiver from her hand and put it on the cradle.

"Not now," he said.

Regina saw the bloodied flashlight in his hand, stifled a scream. Roger shoved the flashlight end under the gushing tap of the kitchen sink, watched the red swirl go down the drain until it was clear. He grabbed a handful of paper towels, held them under the cold water, then said, "Follow me."

He led the way to the basement.

"Please don't scream," he whispered to Regina's terrified face.

He opened the door, let himself and Regina in, closed the door behind them. She was staring at Greco, sprawled.

Roger stooped, tried wiping the blood from Greco's face with the wet paper towels.

"Is he breathing?" asked Regina.

"I don't know."

"Mouth to mouth," said Regina.

"What?"

"Resuscitation."

Roger looked at the face. "I couldn't." And, as if in explanation, "He tried to knife me. He threatened to come back and take Nancy."

Regina, as if she hadn't heard, kneeled, and, placing herself, closed her eyes, put her lips against the black boy's mouth, and began a steady deep-breathing rhythm, as she had learned in first-aid class.

Disgust churned Roger's stomach. He picked up the kilo Greco had dropped, went up the stairs, and out the back door. In Greco's car, Matilda sat behind the wheel.

Roger shoved the kilo at her through the window. "Greco said to take this and get out of here fast."

"Where is he, Mr. Maxwell?"

"He said to do that now. He said you'd know where to go."

Matilda put the kilo on the seat beside her, thought better of it, turned the ignition off, and went to stow it in the trunk, where she wrapped both kilos in a dirty blanket. Roger waited till she drove off.

When he came into the boiler room, Regina lifted her head from Greco's mouth. Her own face and hair were clotted with streaks of blood.

"I think he's dead," she said.

8

JEB DECIDED that the Bestiary Room was too crowded. He ordered Dorry and his friends to take their things to Dorry's bedroom on the second floor.

"Mom said the Bestiary Room is for all of us," said Dorry.

Jeb sat up on his bunk bed. "Hey, Donald, who's this kid talking back to me?"

"He's supposed to be your brother."

"You mean my baby brother?"

"I guess."

"You think he's looking for trouble?"

"I think he's found trouble," said Donald.

"Were you going someplace?" Jeb asked Dorry.

Kenny grabbed Dorry's arm. "Come on, let's go."

"All right," said Dorry. "It stinks here anyway."

"It won't stink no more as soon as you're out the door, wise-ass," said Jeb.

"Meat stinks when it's twelve years old," said Donald.

"Cheese stinks when it's twelve years old," said Jeb.

"You think they're twelve years old?" asked Donald.

The three twelve-year-olds skulked off, Dorry leading the way. Jeb slid off the bunk onto the floor with a thump, and closed the door of the Bestiary Room behind them.

Donald laughed.

"Now," Jeb said, "we can talk."

"I suppose that's the end of the grass," said Donald.

"Oh, Greco'll come up with someplace else. He says whenever it's stashed one place, he's got the next place picked out so's he can move it fast if he has to."

"What place has he got next?" asked Donald.

"He didn't say."

"I thought Greco was your buddy."

"He doesn't tell me everything. I don't tell you everything."

"You told me about Matilda," said Donald.

"That's so you'll find some for yourself. Give your hand a rest," said Jeb.

"Go to hell."

"You recommending it from personal experience?"

Jeb hoisted himself back onto the bunk.

"How come she puts out for him?" asked Donald.

"You got something against putting out?"

"I mean she's . . . you know . . . and he's . . ."

"He's hung." Jeb spread his hands to indicate size.

"Greco let *you* ball her, smallcock, so *he* looks good?"

Jeb swung his legs off the bunk bed.

Quickly Donald said, "I was only kidding. You ever over to her place?"

"Sure. You wouldn't believe it. Her old man comes home from work—I was there once, boy—plunks himself in front of the TV, eats whatever the kids give him, falls asleep in the TV chair. The kids drag him upstairs, he's so zonked he can barely walk."

"What happened to Matilda's mother?"

"She's dead, dope."

"How come?"

"She says he killed her."

"Who says?"

"Matilda, idiot."

"Why isn't he in jail?"

"How should I know, stupid? Matilda just doesn't want to be next. That's why she lives over at Greco's place mostly."

"Was it good?"

"Was what good?"

"You know—Matilda."

"All right."

"How come Greco let you?"

"I'm his friend."

"I'm his friend, too," said Donald.

"It was part of the deal for keeping the stuff here."

"Does that mean he won't let you no more?"

"Doesn't bother me. Plenty around these days. You ought to try it."

"What makes you think I haven't?" said Donald.

"You wouldn't know what one looked like if you didn't see pictures." Jeb put his hands behind his head. "Don't worry," he told Donald, "I'll fix you up soon."

"I don't need you to fix me up."

"Suit yourself." Then, "Come on, I'm feeling restless. Let's see what's doing downstairs."

With gentleness Roger said to her, "Regina, you don't want the children seeing that blood on you. Let me help you wash yourself in the kitchen sink."

"I'll do it," she said, turned on the water hot and cold, bent over the sink like a crone, cupped her stiff hands under the faucet's splash, brought the lukewarm water to her face. *It's all over.*

With paper towels, she dried hands that looked to her like wax claws.

Roger wanted to succor her.

"You'd better call the police," she said.

"Yes," he said.

He went to the phone.

She looked at him. It would be easier if she left the room. It was a private call.

Roger pulled a chair over to the kitchen phone. The dizziness would go away.

Regina heard him dialing as she went to sit in the living room and wait.

The same number summoned the police and the volunteer ambulance. It was too late for the ambulance, though he supposed they would send it for the body eventually.

"Sergeant Whitely," the voice answered.

He tried to picture Sergeant Whitely. Was he the shorter one who wore his hat soft on the sides and waved the housewives on in the morning as they dropped their husbands at the train station?

"Sergeant Whitely," said the voice again.

He should have formulated what he would say. It would matter later. Should he say there'd been an accident?

There was a click. The line was dead. Why did he hang up so soon? Busy? Or did the Sergeant suspect a breather? A breather wouldn't call the police. Don't they try to trace the calls? It couldn't be worth the effort.

Wearily, he went into the living room.

"Did you call?" Regina asked.

He nodded. It wasn't really a lie. He had called. He just hadn't been able to speak right then.

"Come sit by me," she said. "While we wait for them."

"All right."

Roger remembered something Cargill had once told him.

It's not the facts of a case that counted but how good the lawyer was. He shouldn't need a lawyer for simple self-defense.

"Greco wasn't an intruder," he said out loud.

"What do you mean?"

"He was an invited guest. Will that make a difference?"

"Difference in what?"

"What the police do."

When the shrill phone rang, Roger, about to put his arm around Regina, reacted like a spastic. They could hear footsteps bounding down the stairs.

They hurried to the kitchen, but Jeb, Donald right behind him, had grabbed the phone.

"Hello?"

Jeb listened, then said, "Just a minute." He put his hand over the mouthpiece. "It's Greco's old man. He said for Greco to get his ass home fast."

"Well, don't just stand there," said Roger, "find him."

Jeb said into the receiver, "I'll go get him. Hang on." As he put the phone down, he noticed how his mother looked. He glanced at his father. Had they been fighting? He galloped off, Donald following.

Roger wondered why Regina was looking at him like that. He couldn't tell Jeb what had happened, with Greco's father waiting on the line. And Donald right there.

"What'll we do?" asked Regina.

Roger put a finger against his lips, pointed to the phone.

"I'll make some coffee," he said.

Regina took the pot out of his hand. "Here, let me do that."

Roger glanced at the phone lying beside the cradle on the counter. Suppose it was Greco's father calling him to say Jeb was dead, would he believe self-defense? Black people murdered each other all the time. Would Jeb have hidden huge quantities of contraband in someone's house? Would his own son come at someone with a knife meaning to use it?

Jeb came down the stairs two at a time, breathless, went out the back door, came back, said, "Can't find him anywhere. His car's not out back. Matilda's gone, too."

"Well, tell him," said Roger.

Jeb picked up the phone. There was a humming on the line. "He must've hung up."

Regina was cleaning up the breakfast table, setting out two coffee cups.

"You sure left a mess in the kitchen," Roger said.

"Not me," said Jeb. "Dorry and his friends made the mess."

"All right," said Roger. "Go cut the grass."

Jeb looked at his father as if he were crazy. "We did the grass yesterday, Dad."

"Well, go on about your business."

Jeb's departing shoulders shrugged. There's just no accounting for the unreasonableness of parents.

A fan whirred in the blower over the kitchen stove. Roger felt Regina's hand on his arm.

"Why don't we wait in the living room?" she said.

He turned to face her. A wife can't testify against her husband. All the same, she would have to explain what she knew. What did she know?

"Regina?"

"Yes?"

"You saw Greco threaten me with a knife when he wanted to get back into the house?"

"I don't think you should talk about it when you're so upset."

"He had a second kilo stashed behind the boiler in the basement."

"Please, you just come into the living room now," she said.

"He's a drug dealer."

"I know, dear. Come."

"In the basement, he came at me with that knife again, and all I had was the flashlight, I mean I—"

"Wait'll the police get here. You'll tell it to them."

"It was self-defense."

"Yes, dear."

They sat in the living room.

"If we just hadn't moved here," said Roger, "Jeb wouldn't have made friends with Greco."

"You just can't let yourself think that way, you hear?"

"It's this house. That crazy room upstairs. Simeon King is a jinx."

Regina took his hands. "It's too late in our lives to get superstitious now. We're caught in a very unfortunate circumstance. We'll deal with it. Together." Then realizing she didn't have confidence in her own words, she blurted out, "Why are they taking so long?"

"I'll call again."

Cargill was right. If you didn't protect yourself in this world, you could be hurt for what you didn't do. Even for what you didn't intend to do. He couldn't let himself drift like this; he had to do something.

On his way to the kitchen, he remembered Gordon Tillings's advice: *I'll take care of your tax problems, update your will from time to time, and help set up your estate, but if you and Regina ever decide to get divorced, I'll tell you where to go. Neither I nor my partners want to handle that kind of work. And if one of the kids gets into serious trouble you should get onto George Thomassy. That son of a bitch is next door to infallible. I've watched him through dozens of cases. He knows criminal law like nobody else around here, and uses his knowledge to get around it for the benefit of his clients. The D.A.'s all know he's a magician in the courtroom, which is why he gets so many cases quashed early. I'll tell you some-*

thing else about Thomassy. He's single and he's single-minded. He enjoys winning. If I was ever in a jam, I'd get Thomassy aboard fast.

Roger quickly thumbed through the phone book, found Thomassy's number. *That's what a lawyer's for, isn't it, winning?*

Four rings went by before a woman's voice answered.

"Mr. Thomassy's office."

Damn answering service.

He tried to keep his voice businesslike. "I need to reach Mr. Thomassy right away. Can you give me his home number? It's not in the book. It's . . ." He hesitated. "An emergency." He felt his voice slipping. She was turning him down.

"Okay, look, have him call me" He gave her the number. "Roger Maxwell, two '1's. He knows me. I know it's a weekend. If he checks in from anywhere, tell him to call me collect. It's urgent."

Stupid answering service. He hung up.

In the living room, he told Regina, "They'll be here soon."

"Roger, I love you."

She always said it that way before saying something she found difficult to say to him.

"Roger, you're an honest man. You've never had a poker face. I can tell when you're lying."

"Lying about what? You heard me on the telephone."

"You didn't call the police."

The dike in his head broke. Regina embraced him as he sobbed.

9

NANCY AND BERNICE were now three-quarters of a mile from the Maxwell house, farther than Nancy had yet had a chance to venture on her cookie-selling missions. Several people had not been at home. One man had answered the door and said he and his wife both had dreadful colds and Nancy and Bernice had better come back some other time.

"I didn't think they're that sick," said Nancy, after the man had closed the door.

"He sounded sick," said Bernice.

"Well, I'm not going to let him pretend to be sick the next time." She made a note of the address on her little pad. They had sold only six bags of cookies at a dollar a bag this trip, the lowest number yet, and Nancy had wanted to show Bernice how profitable it was. The ingredients for all the cookies had cost a dollar forty-three, and they still had eight bags left.

"You know," said Nancy, as they sauntered into thus far unproved territory, "next time I'm going to put one less cookie in each bag."

"Won't that be cheating?"

"I don't tell how many cookies. I just call it a bag."

"But the people who bought cookies before, they *know* how many are in a bag."

"Oh, Bernice, you're just ridiculous. Nobody counts the cookies. They just eat them one at a time."

They stopped in front of a two-story brick house. The illegible name on the mailbox out front looked like it had been defaced a long time ago. The front door had a sign on it. Closer, they could make out the words: NO SOLICITING.

"What does that mean?" asked Bernice.

"I guess it means we go around the back."

"You sure?"

"Sure I'm sure."

"Where's their car?"

"Not everybody has to have a car. Maybe they walk. They probably keep it in back."

Nancy pointed to a driveway down the road. "That must go around the back."

Bernice seemed skeptical. "Wanna bet?"

"Bet what?"

"It's just an expression," said Bernice.

"That's no bet."

"Penny?"

"Penny's no bet."

"Dollar?"

"Oh, all right," said Nancy, thinking she really needed to get a new best friend who wasn't a slave like Bernice.

At the driveway, they tried to make as little noise as possible on the gravel.

"They'll hear us," said Nancy, stepping onto the grass.

"They'll get mad if you walk on the grass."

"What they don't know won't hurt them," said Nancy. As far as she was concerned, Bernice was finished.

The driveway curved in the direction of the brick house. Beyond a hedge, a brick garage stood separate from the house.

"I win," said Nancy. Just then a dog barked and the side door of the house opened. A mummy stood behind the dog, all taut skin and veins.

"She must be a hundred," whispered Bernice.

"What are you two doing there?" called the woman, stretching the power of her frail voice.

"We're selling cookies," said Nancy. "They're cheaper than Girl Scout cookies, and a lot better. Want to taste a sample?"

When the dog came forward, it seemed to have the woman on a leash.

"Can't you read the sign?" asked the woman.

The girls, afraid, stood silent as the dog growled. It had big teeth.

"Well, if you can't read, at least you could knock on the front door stead of sneaking around."

"We'll know better next time, ma'am," said Nancy, staring at the dog's teeth.

"Be no next time," said the woman. "Don't want no trespassers at my age. Now git."

Nancy and Bernice fled back along the gravel path to the street. As soon as they were out of sight, they were laughing.

"Oh, is she decrepit," said Nancy. "Oh, is she old."

"You going to go back sometime?" asked Bernice.

"Sure will. With a free cookie for the dog. Free rat-poison cookie."

"What do you mean?"

"You really don't understand anything, do you? My dad keeps little round things with rat poison in the basement. One of those would make a whole bag of poisoned cookies. I'd give it to her for fifty percent off. She couldn't refuse."

"But the dog would die."

"You saw the way he growled at us. He deserves to die."

"Suppose the woman ate one of the poisoned cookies?"

"She's too old to live anyway," said Nancy, skipping on the sidewalk.

Together they went up to the front door of the next house.

"You must call the police. Roger." said Regina. "There's just no other way."

"I have to talk to a lawyer."

"You could call Gordon Tillings."

"No," said Roger.

"Do you think . . ." said Regina.

"Think what?"

"Think you need a—" she hated the word—"a criminal lawyer?"

He stared at her.

"If there's going to be any kind of problem, Roger. you remember Gordon said a man like Thomassy. I mean, he's not like Gordon is socially, but they say . . . you know what I mean."

"I've already called Thomassy," said Roger. "I'm waiting for him to call back."

Jeb huddled his body over the extension phone in the library. On the two occasions when he had picked up Greco at home Greco's father. taller than Greco, had tolerated his son's friend with a wave Jeb hoped was friendly. That man's black expression reminded him of how he'd felt when he'd gotten into that empty elevator in Sears's parking garage in White Plains and three black men had come in after him just before the doors closed. They had stared at him. There was nowhere to run. It turned out they didn't do anything but he was greatly relieved when the slow elevator finally rose to his floor and the doors opened. He wouldn't want to cross Greco's father. He wouldn't want to get Greco in trouble with his old man either.

The black woman who answered the phone said, "I git him," when he asked for Greco's father. Did she know he was white from his voice?

It took a long minute till Greco's father came on. "Who want to talk to me?"

"This is Jeb Maxwell."

"What you leave me hangin on the phone so long for?"

"I couldn't find him."

"Matilda say he there. Matilda say somethin bout some trouble wit your old man."

Jeb scrunched himself farther into the chair.

"You there." Greco's father snapped.

"I'm here," said Jeb.

"You listen. Matilda brought two kilos back. I *know* there were three. You tell Greco he don't bring the third one home right now. I'm gonna have his hide, understand?"

"I can't find him."

"What you mean you can't find him? He's there, ain't he?"

Jeb didn't know what to say.

"Listen, you tell that boy I'm coming over to git him and that kilo both."

Jeb turned to see his mother, her hands clasped in a way that always meant she wanted to talk to him. How long had she been standing there?

"Your father wants to talk to you."

"Me?"

"All of us. That is, Dorry and you and me."

"What about Donald?"

"No, just the family."

"Where?"

"Upstairs. In our bedroom."

Regina, Dorry, and Jeb sat on the king-size bed. Roger turned from the picture window and addressed them.

"This is a family conference," he said.

"Nancy's not here," said Dorry.

"She's out selling cookies with Bernice," said Regina. *Thank heaven.*

"I'm sorry we can't do this in the living room," said Roger, "but there isn't a closed door, it's not very private. We have guests this weekend, and what I'm about to say is for the family only."

Roger coughed into his hand. "Something has happened that affects all of us, which is why I have convened you."

"What does convened mean?" asked Dorry.

"Gathered," said Jeb, watching his father.

"We have gathered," said Roger, "because in a crisis, whether it's a crisis of health or money or accident, a close family sticks together."

Jeb wished his father would get to the point. Donald must be wondering what the hell was going on.

"Mother and I planned a special weekend for you, one in which you could bring your best new friends to the house for a sleep-over, have them participate in our family picnic, go swimming with us, share our meals. As you," he was looking straight at Jeb, "and Dorry know, the weekend started getting a bit out of hand on the very first night. Mother and I did nothing to let it get out of control—in fact, the opposite. And though none of you, including Nancy, behaved perfectly, I think the mere presence of your friends—"

"Roger," said Regina, "I think you'd better get to the point."

"Yes. There's been an accident."

"What accident?" Jeb was standing.

"Sit down, Jeb. Your friend Greco made something available to you that is forbidden both by law and in this house. I told him to leave. Then it turned out that for some time— I don't yet know how long, and I need your cooperation to find out—he's been hiding huge quantities of marijuana in this house. He had a whole kilo hidden in the Bestiary, and when I followed him to the boiler room, where he had hidden another kilo, he did something . . . well, he threatened me with a knife, a switchblade knife."

Jeb was standing again when the bedroom phone extension rang in the small box against the far wall. The first thought that occurred to Jeb was that Greco's father was phoning again. He picked up the pink telephone set in his left hand, took the receiver off with his right, and suddenly realized that the wire from the phone hung loose, that it wasn't connected to the wall. The phone rang a second time.

Roger was already on his way out the bedroom door, followed by Regina, saying over her shoulder, "You both stay right there, you hear?"

In the kitchen, Roger picked the receiver off the cradle, steadied his hand, then put the receiver to his ear, saying "Yes" in the most ordinary voice he could summon.

"I have a collect call for anyone from Harry Maxwell. Will you accept the charge?"

Harry! "Yes, operator," Roger said.

"Go ahead, please."

"Hi, Dad." The operator's voice had sounded close. Harry's sounded distant.

"Where are you?"

Harry gave a half-laugh. "As a matter of fact, I'm in a police station in Brattleboro."

Roger looked at Regina over the top of the phone. "It's Harry" was all he said.

"I'm in trouble," said Harry.

"What did you do?" He knew Harry would get his license suspended some day.

"Hey, Dad, please, a friendly voice is what I need right now. There's been an accident. In the Austin."

"Are you all right?"

"Yes and no."

"What the hell is that supposed to mean?"

"Hey, Dad, please, I've got two cops standing over me. It took nearly half an hour to get them to let me place this call."

If you can talk, thought Roger, *you're in a lot less trouble than we are here. I have to force my voice to say words.*

He could hear Harry saying "Okay, okay" to someone at the other end. Then, "Dad? I was with a girl. From school. The Austin hit the tree on her side. She's in the hospital. They're working on her. Dad, I hate to ask this, but could you drive up here now?"

"Harry? That's six or seven hours."

"They say they're holding me on a charge."

"Were you drunk?"

"Dad, I had two beers. You know I wouldn't drive if I'd been drinking."

"Then why are they holding you?"

"They said they always hold the driver while any occupant of the car's being patched up in the hospital. To see how the injured comes out, I guess."

"On what charge?"

He could hear Harry swallow before answering.

"Reckless driving." Then he quickly added, "They say that's because no other car was involved in the accident. We just ran into the tree."

"I don't see how—"

"Dad, they're not going to let me talk much longer."

"You reversed the charges."

"They say it's tying up the phone. Dad, I really can't talk freely. I need you up here."

"Let me talk to one of the officers."

He could hear the phone being handed over, then a New England voice saying, "Sergeant Bledsoe."

"Sergeant, this is Roger Maxwell, the boy's father. Why is he being held?"

"Mr. Maxwell, we suggested to him he could hire a local lawyer, gave him the names of five or six around here, but he won't talk to any of them until he's talked to you. Here he is again."

"Just a minute, Sergeant—" But it was no use. Harry was on the line again.

"Dad, it's really impossible to talk about on the phone. Can't you come up?"

"Harry, you must tell me what happened."

"I will, privately, when you get up here. Please?"

"Harry, I can't drive up."

"Dad? Don't hang up! Look, Dad, this girl Susan who's in the hospital, she's a very sophisticated girl—I mean, sexually . . ." It had been the hardest word to get out.

"You were driving?"

"It's very hard to explain."

A moment of silence.

"Dad, all these lawyers are local people. I'm not sure they'll understand, I'm not sure anyone will. I just have to have someone from the family to help decide what to do, and it can't be Mother because—well, the circumstances, don't you understand? Besides, she wouldn't drive all that distance alone, you know that."

"I'll wire some money," Roger said.

"That's not the problem. Dad? Please?"

"It isn't a matter of wanting to. It isn't possible for me to drive up there now, Harry. I'd do anything to help you but I can't right now."

Harry's voice sounded hollow. "I never thought you'd let me down. Please let me talk to Mother."

Roger, severed from his oldest son, handed the phone to Regina.

"Harry," she said, "what's happened to you?"

"I explained to Dad. I really can't talk much longer. I'm in a jam. The Austin's wrecked. The girl I was with is in the hospital. Dad's got to call the insurance man and come up here and advise me about a lawyer and what I can—are you there?"

Regina held the phone away from her when she heard a scream lance its way up from the basement.

"What's that?" said Harry from the phone.

Roger's face went dead gray. From the basement, he could hear Jeb scream again and again, and then the footsteps of others—Donald? Dorry and his friends?—rattling down the stairs.

Regina put the phone next to her ear.

"Jesus Christ, what's happening there?" pleaded Harry.

"Oh, Harry, baby, we're in terrible trouble here," his mother said.

Those are the last words Harry heard in Brattleboro before the line went dead. Roger had taken the receiver from Regina and put it down on the cradle.

"You've got to go down there," said Regina quietly.

"I know."

Then the phone rang.

"Let it ring," said Roger.

"Suppose it's Mr. Thomassy," said Regina.

The phone rang a second time.

"It's just Harry trying to call back. Let it ring."

She wished Roger would go.

He watched her temptation as the phone rang yet again. He shook his head. The minute Roger left the kitchen for the back stairs, Regina picked up the receiver, but the phone had gone dead. Whoever had been calling had given up.

She followed Roger down to the basement, her life uncurling like a ball of twine unraveling out of control.

10

THEY WERE ALL THERE, the mourners, around Greco's corpse, Jeb, Donald, Dorry, Kenny, Mike. The three youngest stared in horror, fascinated. Greco's face had grayed, as if a thin powder of fireplace ash had been dusted over its blackness. Donald was trying to comfort Jeb, as if he were the closest to the deceased. Jeb, his chest heaving, exhausted by his screams, turned to watch his mother and father come into the boiler room.

"Dad will explain what happened," said Regina, stepping forward to put her arm around her grieving son, but Jeb, his eyes red with crying and anger, flung off her arm as if he would be contaminated by it.

"You don't understand," said Regina.

"You've been saying I don't understand all my goddamn life," Jeb said. "I'm not a little kid any more. I dig a lot more than you think I do. I know about him."

"He's your father!"

"That doesn't give him any right, he can't go around killing anybody he can get his hands on, just because he doesn't like them or something, can he, can he?"

Dorry said, "He hurt Greco too hard."

Roger, his heart pounding, shut the basement door behind him. "Let's try to deal with this rationally," he said.

"I don't give a shit about rationally," said Jeb.

"Your father is waiting for a call-back from a lawyer," said Regina.

"I don't give a shit about lawyers!"

"Don't talk that way," said Regina.

"He killed Greco. He's a murderer!"

"It was self-defense," Regina pleaded.

Roger moved a step forward. Dorry and his friends went around behind Jeb. Were they seeking his protection, siding with him?

"Jeb," said Roger. "Please understand, he was coming at me with—"

"You've been going for *him* all weekend! Everybody here saw you going after Greco," Jeb shouted. "Do this, do that, clean up, straighten up, mow that, do, do, do, as if we're your slaves!" His voice rose. "You don't give a shit what happens to us as long as you have your way."

My son will testify against me. He will persuade his friends to testify against me.

"Jeb," he said, "all of us have been visited by this unfortunate accident. If in our anguish we do the wrong thing, nothing can rectify the further harm we'll do to each other. There'll be no family left. Where are you going?"

"I'm going to the neighbors."

"No, you're not."

"I'm going to call the police."

"Mother will call the police." He had his hand on Jeb's shoulder.

"Get your hand off of me. You're a fucking murderer!"

Roger pulled his hand off Jeb. His back was up against the door.

"Get out of my way!" said Jeb.

For the first time in his life, Roger was frightened of his own son. He'd have to do something quickly. "Regina," he stammered, "for, for God's sake, stand where I'm standing, for two minutes, please!"

She wouldn't refuse him, she took his place as he let himself out the door and pulled it tight against the jamb.

"Hurry!" she said.

"Mother, please get out of the way."

"Jeb." Her voice, though quivering, had a strength she summoned rarely. "Let the grownups handle this."

"Donald," said Jeb, "help me get my mother away from that goddamn door."

Donald shook his head.

"Please," said Regina, "no more violence."

"Tell that to him! Dad was out to get Greco!"

"That's not true. The truth is Greco had kilos of marijuana stowed away in this house."

"Oh, Mother, so what?"

"It's illegal. He's a dealer and you knew it."

"Murder isn't legal."

"Your father didn't murder anybody. Greco tried to stab him."

"I don't believe that! I never saw Greco hurt anybody." Drained Jeb realized his lie. He had seen Greco in action with kids who hadn't paid up in time.

"We're all in this together," said Regina.

In the pantry, Roger hurriedly rummaged through the miscellaneous hardware he had collected over the years, and found the hinged hasp and padlock he was looking for.

Armed with a screwdriver, Roger descended the cellar stairs, holding the hasp. He could hear the voices inside the boiler room. He worked quickly, mechanically, four screws in one side, two on the other. Each of the screws got one last twist for good measure.

"Regina," he called.

"Yes?"

"Come out here." He opened the door for her. The minute she was out, he jammed his full weight against the heavy door, had her stand with her back to it. Roger closed the hasp, put the padlock on, locked it, pocketed the key.

"Okay," he said.

Just as Regina moved away from the door, there was a crash against it from the other side.

"That won't give," said Roger. "It's a very strong door. They'd have to break the jamb away from the wall."

The phone rang in the kitchen. "Please get it," said Roger, dashing up the stairs. "I've got to check the outside cellar door and make sure it's locked."

Regina picked up the phone before the third ring.

"There's your party," said the operator.

Regina heard the sound of quarters bonging, then a dime, then a nickel.

"Go ahead, please," said the operator.

"This is George Thomassy. My answering service said to call Mr. Maxwell urgently."

"Thank you for calling back. I'll get him."

Roger was just coming in from the outside.

"It's locked, all right," he said. "Thomassy?"

She handed him the phone.

"Roger Maxwell," he said.

"I tried earlier," said Thomassy. "There was no answer. I had the operator check the number. What's up?"

"I'm sorry I didn't get to the phone on time."

"I'm up in Danbury, Connecticut, and running out of change."

"We've met two or three times, Mr. Thomassy, perhaps you remember. Gordon Tillings's house? He handles my usual legal affairs. He said you were the best criminal lawyer in the area."

Roger felt Thomassy's impatience humming on the line.

"I've got a problem," said Roger. "I need advice. In your area of specialization."

"I don't specialize. Crime is crime. If you'll call my office Monday morning, my secretary will be glad to make an appointment."

"It's quite urgent. You see . . ." He didn't know how to explain it on a telephone.

"I'm calling from a phone booth, Mr. Maxwell, and I've used up most of my coins."

"Please don't hang up."

"Mr. Maxwell, why the rush? On Monday . . ."

"Look, this'll probably sound very strange to you, but there's a dead boy in the basement."

The operator was back on the line. Had she heard?

"Your three minutes are over. Signal when you're through."

"Operator," said Thomassy. "I can't put dollar bills into this thing and I'm nearly out of change."

"Operator," said Roger, "can we reverse charges for the rest of this call?"

"Why don't you just hang up and place the call from your end?"

He couldn't tell her he was afraid that Thomassy, annoyed, wouldn't be there. *I don't know the phone booth number.*

"What number are you calling from?" asked Roger.

"Operator," said Thomassy. "I can't make out the number. Vandals have been in here and the number's all crossed out.

Would you please"—there was unbending authority in his voice—"charge the balance of this call to the party in Westchester or give me your supervisor."

"I'll charge it. What's the number you're calling?"

"You have the goddamn number. I gave it to you when I placed the call!"

"You dialed zero and the number."

Roger gave the operator his number.

When she got off the line, Thomassy said, "You were saying?"

"Dead boy in the basement."

"I heard that. Tell me the circumstances. Just the facts."

"I had . . . well, you see, I had . . ."

"Yes?"

"I believe I killed him."

"An intruder?" asked Thomassy.

"He was staying here. Visiting one of my children. Look, this is no boy, he's . . . he was . . . nineteen and black. He pulled a knife on me. It's hard to explain. You see he was hiding large quantities of narcotics in my house . . ."

"What was he hiding?"

"Marijuana."

"Marijuana, Mr. Maxwell, is not a narcotic."

"But it's illegal. He was a dealer. He made sales right at my front door."

"How long has this been going on?"

"Mr. Thomassy, can you come over?"

"I'm pretty nearly an hour away. Listen, Mr. Maxwell, what you're saying isn't too clear. Have the police been there yet?"

"I haven't called the police."

"Why the hell not?"

"I wanted to talk to a lawyer first."

"Look, Mr. Maxwell, I'm stacked up to my ass in cases

right now and you need someone right away. Take these names and numbers down. They're all good men in the area and one of them can help you."

"I want you, Mr. Thomassy. I can't afford to chance being convicted."

"I can't afford to lose weekend time. The young lady I'm with is not always available."

"I'll make it worth your while. Two thousand dollars as a retainer."

"I don't remember your occupation. You're a—"

"Banker." The word sounded funny.

"What bank?"

He told him. And his position. "You see," Roger said, "a scandal would make life impossible."

"When did this happen?"

Roger glanced at his watch. "Nearly an hour ago."

"Christ! And you haven't called the police?"

"I need advice. Because of the circumstances."

"What circumstances?"

"It was self-defense."

"Then what are you worried about?"

"I'll make it five thousand."

"Up front?"

"Up front."

He could hear Thomassy open the door of the phone booth. "Honey," he said, "five thousand dollars if you and I take a rain check." Roger couldn't make out the rest. Thomassy must have covered the mouthpiece. Then he came back on the line. "Maxwell?"

"Yes?"

Why was the phone so damp?

"It'll take me at least forty—forty-five minutes fast driving to get there."

"I'm so grateful."

"Who's in the house with you?"

"My wife, three of the children, and some weekend guests."

"What kind of weekend guests?"

"Children. I mean friends of my children."

"Christ," said Thomassy, "do they know?"

"I'm afraid they do."

"Do you have a police record? For anything?"

"Of course not."

"No offense. What's your address?"

Roger gave it to him and started his usual directions.

"I know where it is. Now, listen, hold the fort till I get there. I can't advise you not to call the police. You should. But it's up to you."

"I understand."

There was a click on the other end of the line. No good-bye or anything.

"Is he coming?"

Roger nodded.

"How long will it take him to get here?" asked Regina.

"Not too long," Roger lied.

He wondered if he should tell her about the five-thousand-dollar retainer he had promised. Better not.

"I think I'll check the cellar door to make sure it's holding."

In the living room, Regina, who didn't smoke, took a cigarette from the black-lacquered box they kept for guests and lit it. It tasted ridiculous. She snuffed it out and went to the library to call the police.

11

REGINA SAT by the phone knowing that if she picked it up and made the call, it would take one minute and be over with. Her hand was stayed only by the fear that what she was about to do was an irreversible deed.

As a child she had heard Grandfather Marcus Allen say, "Now you be careful, child, if you tell a lie. You can always fix yourself in the eyes of God by repenting and telling the truth, but if you harm someone beyond repair, that's an irreversible deed, and no amount of repentance is ever going to turn an irreversible deed around."

That admonition of childhood had lingered through her life. She had thought of her virginity as something that would be lost as the result of an "irreversible deed." And much later, she had steeled herself for the irreversible deeds that would be announced by phone: Roger had been hit by a truck, a child had fallen from a school window. Regina had imagined a policeman at the door, come to tell her that Roger had succumbed in a gutter somewhere, and she knew that if a police-man came, it would not be to say Roger was in a hospital somewhere being mended but that an irreversible deed had happened. Regina had never before thought of something happening that would cause an irreversible deed to Roger while he remained living.

It *had* been an accident. If Roger hadn't done anything *wrong*, it would be a mistake to delay calling the police, wouldn't it? A delay would seem guilty. Roger's just not think-ing clearly the way he always does, or he'd have called right away himself.

She dialed the police.

Quickly, after the first ring, a voice answered. "Patrolman Beverly."

"I'm sorry," said Regina, "I didn't get your name."

"Beverly," said the voice. He sounded displeased about having to repeat it.

"This is Mrs. Roger Maxwell, Fox Lane." She wasn't be-traying him, afterward he would be glad. It was for their own good.

"Yes, Mrs. Maxwell."

She could hear other phones ringing at his end, and back-ground voices. He seemed in a hurry. He didn't know, of course.

"We need a policeman." She was condemning herself, too.

"What's the trouble, Mrs. Maxwell?"

"I think a police officer had better come here. I really can't say any more. Second house on the right in Fox Lane, the driveway's marked."

She hung up.

They wouldn't not come, would they?

Regina wended her way up the staircase to the second

floor, then along the hall to their bedroom, touching each picture on the left-hand wall as she passed.

She found Roger standing on her dressing-table chair, getting something from the high hat closet.

"What are you looking for, dear?"

He had found it. When he turned, she could see the gun in his hand. Oh, lord, why had he ever kept that thing?

Roger got off the chair, moved it, got on again, rummaged through a shoe box with his free hand, found the clip of bullets, hopped off the chair, shoved the clip home into the gun, put the gun in his pocket.

"What are you going to do?" she said.

He went past her without answering.

"Roger?"

"I heard you call the police."

"I thought that's what I was supposed to do."

"I didn't tell you to do that."

"I was sparing you the pain of calling yourself."

"Thanks a lot."

"Roger, whatever happens, happens to both of us."

"They're coming to get me, not you."

"Please don't put that gulf between *us*." She said "us" as if it were the name of an individual. "Please be rational. All I told them was we needed a policeman at the house."

"I've never been more rational. What will a policeman do?"

"You'll tell him what happened."

"He'll hear what the kids have to say. He'll see the body."

"Roger, please."

"He'll run me in so that all the neighbors'll see."

"They don't have to."

"I'll be fingerprinted, charged, have a record. The newspapers will gobble it up, a banker arrested, it's the end!"

"No it isn't."

"You've killed my position. You've made it impossible for me to go on living in this community. You've killed me!"

He sounded so like Jeb. He even looked like Jeb just then. She closed the bedroom door.

"Roger, please sit down on the bed."

"You should have waited till Thomassy came," he said.

"Put the gun back. You wouldn't use it against another person, would you?"

He looked up at her, a boy ready to cry in her arms. He shook his head.

"Please," she said. "You're not a man who runs away from problems."

Out of the window she could see Nancy and Bernice coming up the driveway, conspiring against the unworthy human race.

"The children are coming," she said, and turned to see Roger's face, drained of its reserves, the eyes socketing fear.

"Hold on to one thing," she said, begging. "You have to act like someone who was involved in an accident. You did nothing that couldn't be helped."

"I . . . I . . . ." Hopeless.

"Please," she said. "For the next few minutes, let me do the talking."

Now, out of the same window, at the other end of Fox Lane, she could see a blue-and-white police car turn the corner.

Regina ran downstairs to the front door, hearing Roger stumbling along behind her, wishing—oh, wishing to God!—he did not have that gun in his pocket.

Nancy and Bernice were just coming up to the door as she opened it.

"Hey, Mom, guess what?" said Nancy, exuberant. "We sold out!"

It took a second for Regina to put in place the memory of Nancy and her friend going out the door with an armload of plastic bags filled with cookies. Now the happy entrepreneur was digging into her pocket to show the money.

The girls turned as the police car wheeled from the paved street onto the crunching gravel of the driveway.

The policeman stopped the car ten yards short of the family group. As the officer swung his bulk from the car, Roger remembered him as one of those who shepherded traffic in the center of town. He was older than most of the men on the force, close to Roger's age, gone to fat, a lazy face wanting the world not to give him any trouble so he could get through his day.

"You the lady who called?"

Regina glanced at Roger's expressionless face.

"Yes," she said.

"What's up?"

"Well, it was . . . look, Nancy, Bernice, go inside, won't you?" She waited till they were inside the door.

"It was a family, you know, squabble of sorts. It's settled now."

The policeman looked at Roger. He didn't look the type to beat up on his wife. That kind lived on the other side of the village, teamsters, yard workers. But you could never tell. Surprises all the time.

"Mind if I go in?" he said.

Roger had to step aside. He wished it were one of the younger policemen; he could handle one of those, make it clear that his presence was no longer needed. But this jowled cop was better handled with the fewest words.

"You," the policeman said to Nancy and Bernice, who hadn't gotten far from the front door, hoping to hear what it was all about. "Young ladies."

They smiled and moved to center stage.

"You all right?" the policeman asked, his eyes right and left inside the door to see what he could see.

"Terrific," said Nancy, not knowing whether she should or should not tell him about her cookie score. Somewhere she had heard that you couldn't sell anything door-to-door without a license. She didn't want to get a license. It was just a waste of money, wasn't it?

"No trouble?" asked the policeman. Usually it was the kids who got the worst if a family argument turned violent.

Nancy looked at her mother. Regina was forcing a smile. Nancy shook her head.

"What about you?" the policeman asked Bernice.

"I'm visiting her." said Bernice.

"Where do you live?" he asked her.

She told him. He nodded. Also a good neighborhood. This house must have cost a fair piece of change, he thought. Wonder what the guy does?

"Excuse me, sir." he said to Roger, "do you work in the area?" Sometimes just stalling brought things out that didn't want to come out.

Roger cleared his throat. "I work in town." He was going to name the bank, decided against it.

"Commuter?"

"Yes," said Roger. "I'm a banker."

The policeman's relief was visible. He'd had lots of unlikelies, as he thought of them, advertising executives, editors, actors, who got into trouble once in a while, but in all his years on the force, he couldn't remember ever having had trouble from a banker type. He'd had a doctor once, a stupid shit on the needle who'd lost the key to his own supply and made so much noise breaking open a cabinet in his own office that someone called the cops. Okay, maybe this banker'd raised his voice. Maybe bankers' wives thought that raising a voice warranted a call to the police.

"If you folks are sure you don't need me. I'll go on." he said, checking them one at a time. "We're here to help," he added, a phrase he found useful. These people would contribute more than average to the Christmas collection this year, he'd bet.

As soon as they were alone in the kitchen, Roger kissed Regina on the cheek.

"Thank you," he said. "Thomassy should be here soon."

12

SLOW DOWN," the woman said to Thomassy. "You're doing eighty."

He glanced in the rear-view mirror. "Not a cop in sight."

"You obey cops," the woman asked, "or the law?"

"What do you think?"

"I think," she said, noticing that he didn't let the accelerator up one hair, "you went to law school to find out how to avoid paying too much attention to the rules other people live by."

Thomassy laughed.

"What the hell are you laughing about?" the woman asked.

"I told you. You act hard-boiled, but you're naïve. Nobody lives by the law. They live by human nature. That's why lawyers make a living, see."

"Please slow down," she said.

He let up on the accelerator. "The 'please' did it."

"You're a gentleman."

"Nope."

The woman knew her relationship with this man in the metallic gray Thunderbird was temporary because all his relationships were temporary. Women were casework to him. She'd never learn enough about his early life to know why.

"Spread your legs a little," he said.

Instinctively, she moved her knees a bit apart.

"Why'd you say that?"

"Just testing."

"What's that mean?"

"See if you'd obey. You did."

"What good that'd do you?"

"I think you know."

"Know what?"

"When a woman becomes obedient, that's a danger sign for me. You warned me about speeding. I warned you. It's called fair play."

"You're a rat," she said.

He glanced at her. She was smiling.

"Most men I've gone with," she said, "are one way before and another way afterward, when they think they own you. You acted that way from the first minute."

"You've got me wrong."

"You're up to eighty again."

"Sorry." He let up on the accelerator. "I just make sure from the start that you don't get things mixed up."

"In what way?"

"Most women I meet think they own you while they're holding you off. I don't think anybody owns anybody."

"Is that why you never got married?"

"Maybe."

"You sure you don't mind if I talk while you drive."

"It's either you or the car radio."

"Shall I turn the radio on?"

"No."

He glanced in the rear-view mirror in the nick of time. The blue sedan was gaining in the outside lane. Unmarked car. Thomassy slowed. He wouldn't have had time to clock me yet.

The woman screwed her head around so she could see what it was. The blue car caught up. The driver was a blond young man, who glanced at them once, and sped by.

"What makes you think he's a cop?"

"His sheriff's hat is in the seat beside him."

"How the hell do you know?"

"It's my business to know. Especially if I like to drive fast. I don't have time for a ticket."

"Why are you taking this goddamn case?"

"I told you. Five thousand bucks."

"You never do anything just for the case."

Thomassy smiled.

"Right?"

"Right," he said. "I like smart women."

"Thank you. You haven't said why you decided to take the case."

"Well," said Thomassy, speeding up when he saw the trooper turn off at the exit, "this banker who called, he's a virgin."

"What's that mean?"

"Guess."

"Don't frustrate me any more. Tell me."

"Most types who need a criminal lawyer have been doing something wrong all their lives, and when they get onto me, it's because they got caught once too often. This Maxwell fellow probably doesn't even cheat at cards. If he plays cards. He's surprised by the trouble he's in. It'll be interesting. I like virgins."

"I'm no virgin."

He rested his hand on her knee for just a second. "I meant in people types, not in women."

"You going to drop me home first?"

"Can't. He's got a stiff in the cellar he can't cope with."

The woman looked at Thomassy's profile. She hoped the affair would last at least a few more times. Most men practically apologized for wanting to fuck her.

In the boiler room, Jeb and Donald tried again and again to push the door open, but the strong lock held.

Kenny and Mike, terrified, were both crying.

"Shut up!" Jeb ordered. Then to Donald, "One more try. When I say three."

At the signal, both sixteen-year-olds lunged at the locked door uselessly.

"That hurt," said Donald, rubbing his shoulder.

"I want out of here," Kenny cried. "I never even saw a body before."

The truth is that all three twelve-year-olds tried to keep their backs to the sprawled corpse, but the temptation of glancing at it was too great.

"Greco looks terrible," said Donald.

"I saw my grandfather," Mike said. "They put make-up on his face. Only the head part of the casket was open. We couldn't see the rest of him."

"Why don't you shut up," said Dorry. He stole a look at the unmoving corpse. "Can't we cover it up with something?"

Jeb was already looking around for the heavy dropcloths the painters had used. They must have taken them away.

"What about this?" asked Donald, pointing to the thin plastic tied down over some unused lawn furniture.

"What's the point?" said Jeb. "You can see right through it. Besides, that thin stuff rips."

"Why don't we turn him over," said Donald, "so we don't see the face."

"Okay. You take the shoulders, I'll take the legs."

"No," said Donald. "I'll take the legs."

"Wait a minute," said Jeb. "The police might not want us touching it."

"When are they going to get us out of here?" Kenny whimpered.

"Now everybody listen," said Jeb. "A body can't hurt you. Watch." He went over to it and touched the part farthest from the face, the foot. It didn't move. He poked it harder. "See," he said, "it's dead."

Jeb stood up from his crouch. "We don't have to worry about what's dead. We have to worry about the others. We've got to make a plan."

"Can't we get out through that crawl space?" asked Donald.

"It doesn't lead anywhere," said Jeb. "Just under the living room and library."

"The cat gets out that way," said Dorry.

"Well none of us is the size of a cat, stupid."

"We could tie a message to a cat."

"We don't have a cat, stupid."

"I know what we could do," Dorry persisted. "We could open the faucet on the hotwater heater."

"What would that do?" asked Jeb.

"There'd be no hot water in the house."

Jeb turned away. It wasn't even worth commenting on, but it had given him an idea. "Hey, Donald, come here." Both boys examined the circuit-breaker panel. "We could shut off all the electricity. That'd get him down here fast."

"But it'd be dark in here," said Dorry.

"I don't want to be in the dark with that thing," said Mike.

"All the electricity goes only if you pull down that main breaker," said Jeb. "If you switch the little ones, you can turn off all the lights except the one in here. Then we can see what we're doing."

"Yeah, but then what are we going to do?" asked Donald.

Jeb spied a box on one of the shelves. Donald helped him lift it down. Inside was the net hammock from the old house.

They spread the hammock out. "I could climb up there," said Jeb, pointing to the top shelf, "and drop it on him as he came in the door."

"Yeah, yeah," said Kenny, anxious for relief from any quarter.

"Suppose he had a gun?" asked Donald.

"I know he's got a gun," said Jeb. "I know where he hides it."

"He wouldn't kill us?" asked Dorry.

"He killed Greco," said Donald. "Why wouldn't he kill the rest of us? The net's no good. He could still shoot."

"Then there's only one thing," said Jeb.

"What?"

"That board."

All eyes turned to the shelf. Next to where the hammock box had been stored lay a length of two-by-four. Jeb took the wood, felt its heft, swung it as they watched.

"A baseball bat'd be better," said Dorry. "I've got one in my room."

"That's a big help," said Jeb. He swung the two-by-four again.

Dorry, suddenly aware of Jeb's intention, said, "You could hide by the door and hit his legs with it."

"What good'd that do?"

"He'd fall."

"And who'd jump him? You? Your friends?"

Jeb swung the two-by-four one more time, decided.

"I'll do it," he said.

"You sure?" asked Donald.

"Help me up."

Jeb put the two-by-four down, climbed on the shelves, helped by Donald.

Crouched on top, he said, "Hand me the wood."

Jeb practiced swinging down, trying to keep his balance. The youngsters watched him, fascinated.

"When?" asked Donald.

"The second he steps past the door. One more try." He swung. "It's hard to keep from falling off."

Jeb motioned for Donald to help him down.

"You sure you want to do this?"

"You got any better ideas?"

"No."

"Come here. See this circuit-breaker panel. When I tell you to, flip all of them except this one marked 'playroom and cellar stairs.' "

"But this is the boiler room."

"They're on the same circuit, idiot. Now help me up again."

Once up on the top shelf, Jeb beckoned for the two-by-four. "Okay," he said. "As soon as I swing, you jump him in case I don't knock him out."

"Me?"

"You. And you little kids help, too. Hold him down if he's conscious till I get help. There are four of you and just one of him."

Donald looked up at his friend. "Suppose you kill him?"

"Just flick the circuit breakers."

"Now?"

"Yes, idiot. Now."

The fluorescent light over the sink blinked and went out. At the same moment, the refrigerator, where Regina was standing, stopped humming. She waited. It did not come back on.

"Roger," she said.

His first instinct was to look at the freezer, which had a red warning light to assure them the connection had not come out of the wall. The warning light was out, but Roger could see the plug still firmly in the wall socket.

Regina tried the overhead lights. Nothing.

"It's the kids in the basement," said Roger. As he hurried to the stairs, the telephone once again demanded to be lifted from its cradle.

13

ROGER STOPPED two-thirds of the way down the cellar stairs, listened to Regina answer the phone.

Regina heard the plonk of large coins, the ping of several smaller ones, then a voice saying, "Mom?"

"Harry, where are you? Why didn't you call collect?"

"I didn't know if Dad would accept the charge. I got five dollars' worth of change from one of the poker players in the station house. Mom?"

Roger started back up the stairs.

In the basement, Jeb crouched on his shelf, feeling the pain of his strained muscles. "Hurry," he said.

On the phone, Harry was saying, "Mom, listen, this is getting serious. The girl, you know, she's in a coma now."

"What girl?"

"Let me have that phone," said Roger. "Please."

Regina shook her head.

"The one who was in the car with me," said Harry.

"Harry, let me talk to those people there. If you've had an accident—"

"It was an accident, I swear."

Roger put his hand on Regina's shoulder. He didn't want her talking to Harry. She might say anything.

"You didn't hit her?" Regina asked.

"Mom, the car we were in was hit by the tree." Harry laughed strangely. "That's almost funny. The tree stood still. The car hit it."

"You were driving?"

"Yes. Sort of."

"I don't understand what that means. Were you hurt?"

"I was very lucky. I've got some contusions on my face, that's all. We hit the tree on the passenger side."

"Weren't you wearing your seat belt?"

"I was, Mom. She wasn't."

"Doesn't the buzzer go off if—"

"The ends were strapped together. She was . . . her weight was on . . . Mom, listen, if Dad's—"

"I didn't hear you, Harry."

"What's that sound at your end?"

It took Harry in Vermont to tell her her own front doorbell was ringing insistently.

"Please get the door," she said to Roger.

"Suppose it's the police again?"

Into the mouthpiece Regina said, "Be right back, hold on, you hear?" She put the phone down, wiping her sweaty hands. She looked down. When had she taken her apron off—she didn't remember. Then the front doorbell again, somebody awfully persistent and rude. She went to get it.

Roger picked up the phone.

"Harry?"

"Dad, what's happening there?"

Roger did not know how to answer that question.

Regina opened the door. George Thomassy's impatience was all over his face.

"Mrs. Maxwell?"

She nodded.

"I'm George Thomassy." He didn't extend his hand.

"Oh, I'm ever so glad you're here, Mr. Thomassy," she said. "Won't you come right in." She glanced at the woman in the metallic gray Thunderbird. "And won't the young lady come in, too?"

"She'll be all right," said Thomassy, stepping past Regina into the house. "She can always drive around if she gets impatient. Anyway, her paperback'll hold her for a while."

"Sorry I didn't answer the door sooner," said Regina, hurrying after him. "I was on the phone. It's my son Harry, he's been in an accident up in Vermont."

"I'm sorry." Thomassy's clipped words seemed not to care. "Where's your husband?"

"He's in jail. I mean my son Harry's in jail. The girl's in the hospital. Can you talk to him? He's on the phone right now."

"I broke off a weekend because your husband said—"

"Please, Mr. Thomassy, my son is desperate."

Thomassy looked at Regina. She could have been attractive to him had she been ten years younger, he thought.

She led the way into the kitchen.

Roger put the phone down, energetically shook Thomassy's outstretched hand.

Regina picked up the phone. "Harry, we're in luck. The best lawyer around here has just come in the front door. Here, he'll talk to you. His name is Mr. Thomassy."

Reluctantly, Thomassy took the phone from her.

"This is George Thomassy," he said into the phone. "What's up?"

Regina observed the lanky man switch the phone from his

left ear to his right. She brought a chair over so he could sit.

They watched Thomassy listening, nodding, reaching into his pocket for a small note pad. He switched the phone back between his left ear and shoulder so he could write.

"Give me the number up there. They got you in a cell?" Thomassy glanced over at the mother. *Boy would she have a fit!*

"Kid," Thomassy said into the phone, "you're lucky it happened in Brattleboro. There's an old fellow up there named Merkin who practices criminal law. Every judge in the area used to work for him at one time or another. Bruce Merkin. Tell him George Thomassy referred you. Oh he'll remember my name. He used to curse it every day of the week during a certain trial." Thomassy laughed. "Tell him everything you just told me. All he's got to do is whisper in a few ears. He'll get you off. Just don't lie to him . . . Hold it a minute."

Regina had touched his sleeve.

"Your mother wants to know who the girl is."

Thomassy listened, then holding his hand over the mouthpiece, said to Regina, "She's not from down here. She's a Providence girl."

Regina said, "Ask him if her family is . . . prominent. Ask him what her father does."

Thomassy asked. Then he said, "All right, kid. Call Merkin. Then call back here when you're off the hook. Your mother's worried about you. I'm not worried. Merkin can't afford to screw up a case I refer to him."

He hung up.

Thomassy looked at Regina, her fingers twisted, waiting for him to talk.

"Look, Mrs. Maxwell, it'll be okay. Her father's nobody special."

"What did Harry do?" She hadn't meant to shrill it. "I'm

sorry," she said. Then, in a more normal voice, "Why are they holding him?"

"Your son is well aware that the mores of the community up there aren't exactly the mores of New York or Fairfield County. Whatever happens to the girl, a good lawyer up there'll just have to make up a story for him that jibes with the facts as the cops know it and sounds reasonable."

"What did he do?"

She wouldn't let him off. "Mrs. Maxwell, you might say he didn't do anything. He was driving. I don't know why he didn't pull off the road, and his girl—I don't know why kids don't hire motel rooms any more—was performing fellatio on him and I guess he got kinda distracted and drove off the road, that's all. Except that the car hit a tree and she's hurt bad. Now let's you and Mr. Maxwell and me sit down somewhere and get to it."

14

I N NANCY'S ROOM, the door shut against the noises of the house. Bernice was saying, "What are you looking at me that way for?"

Nancy pulled the flowered curtains across the double window, and in the half-dark room flicked the light switch. Nothing happened. The bulb needs changing, she thought. Damn! "I'm trying to figure out if I can trust you," she said.

"I'm your friend," said Bernice, her voice a question mark.

"I had a friend in the old neighborhood I couldn't trust," said Nancy with disdain, opening the curtains again so they could see. "She told her mother everything."

"I don't tell my mother things."

"How can I be sure?"

"Cross my heart?" asked Bernice.

Nancy seemed unconvinced. "Why don't you go out in the hall while I hide my money," she instructed.

"Please," said Bernice, "I wouldn't take it. I . . . don't really care that much about money."

"If you're the only one who knows—"

"You can trust me."

"If any's missing, I'll know it's you."

Nancy spread the morning's haul of dollar bills from cookie-selling out on her bed. She knew exactly how much she had saved, how much she added each time. She would be glad if Bernice stole *some* of her money. Then she could get Bernice to do anything.

"I'll show you," she decided.

Nancy pulled the one chair in the room over to the dress closet. From her bookshelf she took an oversized Atlas and put it on the chair seat. Then, one hand braced on Bernice's shoulder, she got up on the chair and opened the foot-high louvered doors over the closet.

"This is supposed to be for hats," Nancy said. "I don't have any hats." From the shelf behind the louvered doors she pulled a rectangular box with Snoopy printed on it. Carefully, she handed it down to Bernice, then climbed off the chair.

"You stand with your back against the door so no one comes in," she instructed Bernice, taking the Snoopy box from her and setting it down on the bed.

"This was a present when I was a kid," Nancy said. "My mother lets me keep my broken souvenirs in it. See." She showed Bernice trinkets and once-precious objects, now destroyed or in disrepair. "She knows I hate to throw things like this away."

From underneath the mess of junk, Nancy pulled a copy of *Harold and the Purple Crayon*. "This isn't it," she said; "it's too small." She took out a second book, *Nancy Becomes a Nurse*. "They gave this to me because the girl's name in it is the same as mine."

Carefully, she opened the cover of the book. Inside, the entire center had been razored out, leaving just the outer margins of each page. In the hollowed-out book was Nancy's treasure, dollar bills, five-dollar bills, and one ten.

"Guess how much I've got in here?" she asked, while adding the bills from the bed to those hidden in the book.

"It looks like a lot."

"It's nearly full. At the bank, people get down on their knees and *beg* my father for money."

"You're making it up."

"Mom took me to the bank. I saw it, cross my heart. If he waves like this—" Nancy gestured grandly— "that means they can have the money. And when he goes like this—" Nancy was a nobleman dismissing a peasant— "they cry. Borrowing is life and death for some people."

"Oh. Nancy!"

"My father is the most important person in the bank." She put her hands on Bernice's shoulders. "Secret?"

Bernice nodded.

"I'm saving so I can have my own bank. You saw how much I have. Does your father have that much money?"

"Not in his pocket, I don't think."

"You see," said Nancy, releasing Bernice. She shut the book and got up on the chair, this time without Bernice's help. She really didn't need help from anyone.

"I can't stay up here forever," said Jeb, the cramp in his calves hurting. "I swear I heard him come part way down the stairs, then go back up."

"I heard the phone," said Donald down below. "And the doorbell."

"Wonder who it is?" said Dorry.

"I hope it's the cops," said Jeb, clambering down.

As Roger led the way into the living room, Thomassy

glanced around the room. He liked the sense of space, the high ceilings, the way the furnishings all tied in with each other. Every woman who came up to his place always bemoaned his hodgepodge collection of things bought at whim. This room looked planned.

Despite the large windows, the lowering clouds outside made the room seem dark. Thomassy wondered why they didn't turn on a light or two.

"Do sit down," Regina said.

"You said"—he turned to Roger—"the corpse was in the basement."

Roger glanced at Regina. "Yes," he said.

"Well, we'll go down there in a minute." Thomassy took his notebook out. "Could we get some more light in here?"

"The circuit breakers have been pulled," said Roger quickly.

Thomassy looked at the nervous man.

"The kids pulled the circuit breakers," said Roger.

"What kids?"

"There are . . ." Roger hesitated, "five of them down there."

Thomassy didn't mind kids one at a time. But five? How careless can you get?

"Only two of them are ours," said Roger. "There's Jeb, and a friend of his named Donald, and Dorry, our twelve-year-old, and two friends of his. All of them are weekend guests—the friends, that is."

"I remember," said Thomassy. "You told me on the phone." He filled his pipe from his tobacco pouch. "It's awfully quiet here for a houseful of kids."

"They're locked in the basement," said Regina, getting it out quickly. "Where the body is."

Thomassy took his eyes off her and looked at Roger.

"It was just until you came," said Roger.

"Whatever for?" asked Thomassy.

"It was necessary," said Roger, leading the way to the cellar stairs.

"I hear someone coming," said Donald.

"Yeah," said Jeb. "Help me up, quick."

Donald boosted Jeb up the shelves until he reached the top, then handed the board to him.

"Don't miss," said Donald.

"Don't worry," said Jeb.

They could hear someone putting a key into the padlock.

"How old are these kids?" asked Thomassy.

"Jeb and Donald are sixteen. Dorry is twelve. His friends are the same age," said Regina.

"Damn this lock," said Roger.

"Anybody else in the house?" asked Thomassy. "A maid?"

"It's her day off. There are two little girls upstairs."

"How little?"

"Nine."

"Jesus," said Thomassy, just as Roger got the padlock open.

Roger removed the padlock from the hasp and stood aside.

Thomassy opened the door, stood just inside the jamb. The boiler room was lit. *These kids are smart.* "You Jeb?" he asked the oldest boy.

Donald had to keep from glancing upward. What if this stranger walked in first and Jeb smashed the board down on his head?

"That's Jeb's friend Donald," said Regina hurriedly.

Thomassy didn't hear her. His eyes took in the three younger boys, standing behind the sprawled black body on the floor. What had he gotten himself into?

Thomassy stepped forward into the room. Donald screamed, "It's not your father!" as Jeb brought the board down hard, trying, too late, to stop its downward course, losing his balance, and falling on Thomassy, caught by surprise, trying to stay upright, then crashing to the floor with Jeb alongside him, as Regina screamed.

"What the hell!" Thomassy yelled at the fallen boy beside him. "Are you crazy?!"

"I didn't know it was . . ."

Thomassy, feeling the pain in his back and shoulder, dusted himself off as he scrambled to his feet. "You trying to kill somebody?" And as he said it, Thomassy realized that the intended victim was probably Maxwell.

"Oh, Mr. Thomassy," cried Regina, "are you all right? Jeb, whatever were you all trying to do? This man is trying to help us. Why did you turn all the electricity off?"

"To try to get me down here," said Roger. "To bash my head in. I was on the way down when Harry called and then the doorbell rang."

"And we'd have had two accidents to deal with," said Thomassy.

"It wasn't an accident," said Jeb.

"You tried to smash my head in with that board," said Thomassy. *"That* was no accident. Now all of you"—he took each of them in with his gaze—"get upstairs to the living room."

They were silent.

"Now."

They didn't move.

"Or I'll have you all hauled in for intent to do bodily harm."

Thomassy stepped aside so the kids could shuffle past him, and up the stairs. He told Roger to turn the electricity back on and come up, then took one quick backward glance at the corpse. *Thank heaven I don't have any kids.*

In the living room Thomassy got them settled on the couch, chairs, and the carpeted floor, designating as much distance as possible between the belligerent kid and his father.

Thomassy did not sit. He paced, letting them stew. Finally, he got his pipe lit again. He had to see who said what first.

It was Jeb who spoke. "I'll tell you everything."

"What everything?" Thomassy approached the chair where the boy was sitting. Jeb stared up at him.

"Were you there when the accident happened?"

"No."

"Okay," said Thomassy facing them all. "Let's get this straight. This matter is going to come before a court of law. I'm an officer of that court and I'm telling you—all of you, including you kids—that there are rules to follow. If you weren't there when something happened, if you didn't see it with your own eyes, everything you say is hearsay, and the judge won't let you talk about what you know secondhand."

He turned back to Jeb. "You understand that?"

"I know what happened!" Jeb burst out.

"You *think* you know, but all you're going to tell me is what you saw and heard. You sit back down. I want to hear your father's story first. He's my client. Then I'll hear you out. Understood?"

And so, in a roomful of strangers, Thomassy let Roger tell what he knew from the moment the visiting children arrived. Once, when Jeb tried to interrupt, Regina placed a cautioning hand on Roger's arm. She let Thomassy silence Jeb, then took her hand off so Roger would continue. She wondered if Thomassy would question her.

It took Roger twenty minutes to tell of the picnic, the events at the swimming pool, the early-morning visitor, the confrontations with Greco.

When Roger finished, sinking back into the pillows, exhausted, Thomassy said, "Thank you. I want to hear from you, Mrs. Maxwell, and from the others, but first I want to ask this young man—Jeb, right?—some questions."

"My father's lying," said Jeb.

"Now you listen to me, young man," said Thomassy. "I'll figure out who's lying and who isn't. Your job is to answer my questions."

In similar circumstances with teen-agers, he had had to slap a face. He couldn't do that with witnesses around, especially the kid's friends and parents. Thomassy loomed over the boy, the pressure of his proximity like a vise.

Jeb glanced at Donald. Could he rely on him?

"Don't look at him," said Thomassy, "look at me. Did you know from firsthand knowledge that this Greco kid was dealing drugs?"

Jeb felt desperate in his isolation.

"Jeb," his mother said, "please answer Mr. Thomassy. Tell the truth."

"I'll know if you're lying," said Thomassy to the boy. "Did you know he was dealing drugs?"

Jeb looked down at his hands. "Yes."

"Yes what?"

"Yes, I knew Greco was dealing."

"Did you report his drug dealing to your parents?"

"No."

"To the police?"

"No."

"Did you know about his drug dealing before or after you invited him here for the weekend?"

"Before."

"And yet you didn't think twice about having him here?"

"He was my friend."

"Friendship aside, did you benefit in any way from his drug dealing?"

"What do you mean?"

"Don't act dumb. Did he give you any money?"

"No!"

"Calm down. Did he give you any dope?"

"Well, I really don't—"

"Tell the truth. Did he give you any?"

"Yes."

"Did you pay him for it?"

"No."

"But what he gave you was worth money, wasn't it?"

"I suppose so."

"You know any place where you can get it free, other than from Greco?"

"No."

"Did you know he was using your parents' house for hiding large quantities of dope?"

"I'm not sure." Jeb glanced at his mother.

"What does that mean?"

"I didn't know how much."

"But you knew he was?"

"Yes."

"And you told no one?"

"No."

"Do you know what accomplice means?"

"Sure I know!"

Regina was on her feet. "Oh, Mr. Thomassy, please!"

Women are a pain in the ass. I'm not going to ask her anything. Thomassy turned to them. "All of you stay put. Don't move." Then, "Mr. and Mrs. Maxwell, you want to step over into the other room for a minute, please?"

Out of earshot of the children, he said, "You hired me to defend you in a serious matter. That boy is very hostile. Lots of kids his age are. A judge might not be as tough on him as I am right now, but we have to be sure that when and if a judge gets to hear his story, what comes out is not some concoction based on a kid's animosity to his old man. He's trying to come on as the total innocent. If he succeeds, your husband'll have a helluva rap to beat. Trust me." He took Regina's hands, not something he liked to do in front of a woman's husband, but it was the right move.

"All right," she said.

Roger took Regina's arm, reclaiming her. They returned to the living room.

"Now I want to make something clear to everybody," said Thomassy. "The first incident, accident, call it what you please, was witnessed by two people, Mr. Maxwell and the boy Greco. Unfortunately, the boy can't tell us anything because he's dead. Mr. Maxwell told us what happened. Now I want to know what happened in connection with the second accident, the one in which the victim was nearly me." Thomassy turned to Donald.

"Tell me what you saw and heard."

Donald's frightened glance was aimed at Jeb. Jeb looked away.

"We've heard from him," said Thomassy. "It's your turn."

At that moment they all heard the sound of girlish laughter from the stairway, and in a moment, with all eyes turned in their direction, Nancy and Bernice stood in the archway leading to the living room.

"We were counting up the cookie money, Mom," said Nancy, wondering why everyone was sitting in a circle and who the man was.

"Nancy dear," said Regina, "this is Mr. Thomassy, a friend of your father's. Mr. Thomassy, this is Nancy and her friend Bernice."

"Hello," said Thomassy. *Christ, more kids!* "Has Bernice been here for the weekend, too?"

Regina nodded.

Roger spoke up. "They are not aware of either event, Mr. Thomassy. Perhaps they are not needed here."

"Girls," said Thomassy, "we're talking about a private

matter. Mrs. Maxwell, would it be all right if they returned upstairs?"

"Nancy," said Regina, "you and Bernice can play in your room."

"I'm hungry," said Nancy.

"Well, take something in the kitchen and then go up to your room."

Nancy was about to say something when she saw how upset her father seemed. She didn't like to see him that way. She led Bernice from the room.

Thomassy waited ten seconds, then turned to Donald again. "The second incident."

"Well we, I mean all the kids, the boys in this room, found Greco and then Mr. Maxwell locked us in the boiler room. Jeb said his father might try to kill us the way he killed Greco—"

"Now hold it!" Thomassy was furious. "You heard every word of what Mr. Maxwell said. Do you think he's a liar?"

"No," said Donald meekly.

"You're not calling him a liar?"

"No, sir."

"You heard Mr. Maxwell say how Greco came at him with a knife and how he protected himself with the only thing he had besides his hands, a flashlight. Did you seriously believe that he would take a flashlight and do anything to you personally if you didn't threaten his life with a switchblade or in some other way?"

"I didn't say that. Jeb said that."

"Said what?"

"Said he thought his father would kill all of us."

"Did it occur to you he might be trying to frighten you?"

"I don't know."

"Did Jeb ever frighten you before that?"

Donald glanced at Jeb.

"Don't look at him. I'm asking you."

"I'm not scared of him."

"But you believed him?"

"I don't know. There was the body."

"Mr. Maxwell said there was a boy here this morning by the name of Tim. Do you know Tim?"

"Sure."

"Is he a friend?"

"Not really, just from school."

"What kind of boy is Tim, do you know?"

Donald squirmed. "He goes with girls a lot."

Dorry tittered.

"Now you keep quiet, Dorry," said Regina.

"What else?" asked Thomassy.

"I suppose . . ." said Donald.

Thomassy waited.

"I suppose Tim smoked dope."

"Do you know where he obtained his dope?"

"I never saw him."

"How do you know he smoked dope?"

"Everybody in school knew."

"That doesn't mean a thing under the law. Did you ever see Tim using dope?"

"Once or twice."

"Where?"

"In school. In the bathroom. He was just showing off."

"Did you know Tim was here this morning?"

"Yes."

"How did you know?"

"Jeb told me he came to get some dope from Greco."

"You shut up," said Jeb.

"I'll ignore that," said Thomassy, keeping his gaze on Donald. "Now tell me about the second incident."

"Well, you see, Jeb's idea was to pull the circuit breakers

except for the one in the room where we were and get his old man, I mean Mr. Maxwell, to come down to the cellar and unlock the door."

"That's not true!" Jeb was standing.

Donald looked bewildered.

"It was Kenny's idea," Jeb lied.

"That's right," said Donald quickly.

"Which one of you is Kenny?" asked Thomassy.

Kenny slowly raised his hand only after everyone looked in his direction.

"All right, Donald," said Thomassy. "Try to remember better from now on. Now, how did Jeb get up onto the top shelf?"

"He climbed up."

"Without help?"

"I helped him get up."

"For what purpose?"

"I don't know," said Donald.

"You do know he was getting up on the shelves, don't you?"

"I guess."

"For what purpose?"

"Look, Mr. . . ."

"Thomassy."

The boy was frightened. Thomassy went over to him and put his hand comfortingly on the boy's shoulder. "Please understand," he said, "nobody is going to hurt anybody from now on. We just want to find the truth, okay?"

Donald nodded.

"What did Jeb have up there?"

Silence.

"You can tell us. We all saw it, remember?"

"A board."

"Why a board?"

"I guess to hit with."

"Hit whom? Me?"

"No, he meant to hit his father."

"But he could have killed me. Were you an accomplice of his in that?"

"No, sir. I didn't do anything wrong."

"You helped him get up there. You didn't try to stop him."

"I can't stop Jeb."

"Well, as a matter of fact, Donald," said Thomassy, the harshness suddenly gone from his voice, "you did stop him when you saw it was me coming through that door. I thank you for that." Thomassy's voice hardened. "But, Donald, if Mr. Maxwell had come through that door, would you have yelled a warning, or would you have let him be hurt or killed?"

As Thomassy had expected, Donald burst out crying. Immediately, Thomassy turned his back on the boy and walked away, thinking he was nearly home. Regina went to comfort Donald.

"I didn't mean to hurt anyone," said the sobbing boy.

Once they're caught at it, Thomassy thought, nobody ever intends anything bad. If you believed newspaper editorials, you thought the world was full of well-intentioned people. Bullshit. George Thomassy was a young kid at the end of the big depression. but he knew that a lot of people were out of work, including his do-gooding father, a social worker without hope. As a sop to the old man, he let himself get misdirected into social work in college. but it stopped him short: that wasn't the way people were. His teachers preached sermons that directly contradicted what he saw and heard. People were the only animals who were vicious to each other without cause. It was a waste of time to look for improvement in the human race. George Thomassy switched into criminal law. It was recession-proof, and nobody ever gave you any lip for winning.

Donald's sobbing seemed under control. Thomassy went

over to where Mrs. Maxwell was providing him with tissues to blow his nose and wipe his tears, and said, "I'm not going to ask you any more questions for now, son."

Thomassy addressed the others, knowing Donald would be listening. "All of you who were down there in the cellar were part of a plan to hurt somebody. That's a very serious thing. Even you"—he directed his attention to the twelve-year-olds— "know inside your own heads that you were in on a plot to harm another human being, and there is no proof that the other human being. Mr. Maxwell, was planning to harm you. In the eyes of the law, you are all just about as guilty as Jeb. You didn't try to stop him. You probably *wanted* to see what happened when that board came smashing down. If I get one of you out of trouble, maybe, with God's help, I can get all of you out of it."

Roger Maxwell stood up. "Are we going to the police station now?"

"Absolutely not. If we go surrender you there, it puts an onus of guilt on you. Let them come here. Let them see you in a family context. Let them take you in. It puts the onus on them. Besides, they'll want to see the stiff."

"The what?" asked Regina.

"The body," said Thomassy. "May I use the kitchen phone?"

"The number's right on the phone below the fire number," said Regina.

"I know the number," Thomassy said. "I work in this community."

15

ROGER STARED at the second hand on his wristwatch, moving in spastic jumps from second to second. Fifteen seconds took an age. Who was that sniffling? Donald? Compared to Jeb, that kid had no guts. Jeb was strong-willed. All kids had some devil in them. It'd be unnatural if they didn't. Time would sort things out. Jeb would mature like Harry, get over his beefs at the adult world. I'll find a way to patch things up between us. When this is over, I'll take Jeb on that trip I have to make to Montreal and Toronto, just the two of us, get reacquainted.

Roger looked up, wanting to say something encouraging to Jeb. He might like to go along on a business trip.

Jeb was facing away.

Roger caught the desolate eyes of Dorry, Kenny, and Mike, bunched together, their twelve years shriveled. Roger wanted to reach out, touch Dorry's head, say *this will pass*. Would he shrink from his hand?

If only they hadn't moved to this unlucky neighborhood.

It was the children wanting this house with the stuffed animals.

The door's bell rang, swiveling all of their eyes in the same direction.

"I'll go," said Jeb.

"Please," Roger said to Regina, "you go."

She stood. I meant no burdens for you, Roger thought.

As if to reassure him, she said, "It couldn't be the police. Thomassy's just phoning." Then she was gone, leaving him alone in a roomful of children he could not talk to, not right now.

He heard Regina saying, "Just a minute," then the heavy front door's creak.

Regina stood in the living-room archway, her face drained. "It's Greco's father," she said. "He wants to know where his son is."

"Sure do," said the large man who had followed her. He was taller and younger than Roger, wore a plaid cotton-flannel work shirt tucked into his overalls.

He nodded at Roger, then at Jeb and Donald. He knew those boys.

At that moment Thomassy returned from the kitchen, in an instant took in the resemblance between the black man's face and the face of the boy in the basement, prudently extended his hand.

"My name's Thomassy."

Greco's father wasn't shaking hands with anybody. "I want to talk to my boy," he said.

The response was silence.

"I knows he's here."

Thomassy gambled. It would be very hard to find out anything afterward. "Mr.?" It was a question.

"Ackers," said Greco's father. "Where's my boy?"

"Mr. Ackers, are you aware your son is involved in this illegal activity?"

"Whatchu talking bout?" Ackers looked at the kids on the other side of the room, then said to Thomassy, "You a cop?"

"No, Mr. Ackers."

"Then what the hell are you talkin bout legal this and that. My son's makin a livin what them kids don't have to do."

"Please, Mr. Ackers," said Thomassy, "I wasn't implying heroin."

"Watch yourself, Mister, I never let my boy handle hard stuff."

"Just grass."

"Where he at?"

"Just grass?"

"I don't have to answer no questions."

"When you set him up in grass, did you think—"

Ackers held up his right hand. "You stop your mouth right now."

"I'll show you where your boy is, Mr. Ackers," said Thomassy, coolly stepping past the raised hand. As Ackers turned to follow him, Thomassy saw the black handle sticking out of the man's overalls pocket. An Afro comb?

A chance he'd have to take.

"Come with me, Mr. Ackers." They all watched Thomassy lead the way to the back stairs.

They waited. Then it came, the primordial cry from the depths of the cellar.

Thomassy watched the overalled man hunched over the sprawled body, his face splayed in sudden anguish like a tabloid photograph. Thomassy steeled himself. He had to think of how to handle the man, how to keep him in check on the witness stand, provoke him to anger, make him snarl, show his potential for violence so the jury could see it!

The man, his eyes blood-veined, stood up.

"Who did it?"

Thomassy knew the benefit, so seldom possible, of catching the bereaved the first minute after death was known. If he put his arm around the stranger, the man would fling it off. He didn't want kindness. He wanted revenge.

"Mr. Ackers, you have my sympathy. Your son was in a dangerous game."

"You . . ." He gasped for a definition of his rage. Thomassy watched Ackers's shoulders, arms, clenching hands. A fury building.

"I said I wasn't a cop, Mr. Ackers."

"You shut yo mouth." The man looked down at Greco, one eye open wide, the other half open, no pupil showing. Ackers bent down to the body again, reached into Greco's left-hand trouser pocket, with difficulty removed a money clip. In it were several large-denomination bills.

"It wasn't for the money," said Ackers. "It was for the hate."

"Try to stay calm, Mr. Ackers," Thomassy said.

Ackers stood up. "Get out of my way."

Thomassy did not move till Ackers's arm shoved him.

"Cool it," Thomassy said, knowing it would have the opposite effect.

Upstairs, they heard the quick clatter of steps. Ackers billowed into the room, his hands flung wide, wailing his rage like the Italian mother in a movie Regina had seen many years ago. Though frightened, she got up to go to him, when his words flung across the room stopped her. "Which one of you did that to my boy?"

Behind him Thomassy said, "I know what a blow this is, Mr. Ackers," and tried to guide him to a chair.

Regina held her hands out toward Ackers, but he spurned her with a rough gesture, his hoarse voice demanding, "Someone did it! I want to know who did it!"

"Perhaps," said Thomassy quietly, "it could be said he did it to himself."

"You crazy, man. You see his head bashed in? How anyone bash in his own head?" His face took in face after face. "Who did it? Who gonna tell my old lady what you did to her boy, who?"

"Mr. Ackers," Thomassy said, "your son attacked Mr. Maxwell with—"

He stopped because Ackers had drawn a knife from his overalls pocket and flicked the blade. "You bastard," he said to Thomassy.

Thomassy now knew everything he needed to know for a courtroom fight. A second-generation dealer. A second-generation knife-fighter.

"I have to warn you, Mr. Ackers," he said, "I've used my judo before with a knife-wielder, and the other fellow lost." It wasn't true, but it gave Ackers a moment's pause.

"Mr. Ackers!" said Roger Maxwell, withdrawing his gun from his jacket pocket.

Dear God, thought Thomassy, *where the fuck did he get that? I've almost won this thing and he's going to blow it!*

Ackers turned to face Maxwell. "This ain't the south, you motherfucker! You can't kill me the way you killed my boy!"

Thomassy's ears, like a hound-dog's searching the air, had heard the car pulling up on the gravel. When the doorbell rang, Thomassy was the only one not startled.

"I suggest you both put your weapons away," Thomassy said. "That's the police."

He went to open the door. The policeman standing there was no more than twenty-two or three, a kid with stonewall gray eyes. *Don't fuss with me,* they said. *Don't give me any of that human-being shit.* Thomassy glanced at the gun holstered on the left side for a quick draw. Too much Steve McQueen watching. Nonnegotiable cops like him don't belong in this part of Westchester.

The police car had pulled up right behind his metallic gray Thunderbird. He could see the woman in it turning to look out the rear window at Thomassy and the cop. Thomassy hoped she had the sense to stay put.

Just then a second police car turned in from Fox Lane onto the driveway. *Damn,* thought Thomassy, *I didn't say felony, I said a death. Why did they send a second car?*

The second car stopped at an angle, blocking the driveway. Out of it came another cop, older. This one was black.

16

W
HEN THE BLACK COP saw the young one he said,
"Hey, Hot Pursuit, who let you out of the station?"

The young one's face flushed. He didn't like being smart-assed in front of civilians. It wasn't his fault he'd chased a ninety-mile-an-hour maniac in an Aston Martin all the way to the Hawthorne Circle and lost him in all those every-which-way clover leafs.

To Thomassy he said, "You phoned?"

Thomassy introduced himself, led them both into the crowded living room. Ackers had collapsed into an armchair, sobbing. His knife was nowhere in sight.

Thomassy glanced at Maxwell. Had he pocketed the gun? He had to get that away from Maxwell somehow.

Roger, hands on knees to keep their shake from showing, looked up at the policeman.

Thomassy had flair. "Gentlemen," he was saying to the police, "this is Mr. Ackers. A bad accident has happened to his son."

Ackers did not look up.

Roger stood when Thomassy, as if it were a grave social occasion, said, "This is Mr. Maxwell, owner of the house. And Mrs. Maxwell."

Regina's nod was barely perceptible.

"The children," Thomassy said, "have some friends visiting."

"Where's the body?" the young cop asked.

"In the basement," said Thomassy. "I'll lead the way."

The moment they were out of sight, Roger thought, *What's to keep me from going out the front door, heading for Canada?* He glanced at Regina.

"Please sit with me," she said, patting the couch beside her.

In the basement, Thomassy watched the cops' expressions when they saw Greco sprawled. The young cop gazed blinklessly. When the black one spoke, he said, "Did this individual" —he pointed at the corpse—"trespass? To your knowledge, that is?"

"This individual," said Thomassy, grateful for the expression, "was a weekend houseguest of one of the older children."

Better lead. They would want to know what a black boy of nineteen was doing with a white sixteen-year-old.

"Officer," said Thomassy respectfully to the black cop, "here's my card. Most of the fellows know me. Mr. and Mrs. Maxwell were not aware that this friend of their son's was a major drug dealer in this area. I think you'll find that his father—that's the man upstairs—is known to be in the business as well. When Mr. Maxwell discovered that the deceased was using the Maxwell residence as a hiding place for large quantities of dope and selling from the premises, he ordered the young man to leave with his . . ." *Use it.* "His white girl friend and the dope. There were at least two kilos. When the deceased went for the second kilo, which he'd hidden in the basement, he threatened Mr. Maxwell with the switch-blade knife that's lying right there. Mr. Maxwell protected himself with the only thing he had in hand, an ordinary household flashlight."

The black officer looked at the body. "I'll have to take Maxwell in. You said the father—the other man—was in on the dope?"

"You'll find a money clip with high-denomination bills in the father's left pocket. He took it off the corpse."

"You saw that?"

Thomassy nodded. "I believe he's also got a matching switchblade somewhere on him."

"Matching what?"

"That one." Thomassy pointed to Greco's knife on the floor.

"There's got to be a complaint," the black cop said.

"I'll sign it," said Thomassy. *Anything for a client.*

"Need to call an ambulance for this," the young cop said. The black one, it was clear, didn't like the other fellow calling the body "this."

"Go ahead," he said. "The detectives'll have your ass."

The young cop's face flushed.

The black one said to Thomassy, "Inexperience, that's all." Then to the cop, "Go get yourself a phone. Tell 'em to send a photographer from the coroner's office. The detectives'll tell you what else to do."

The young cop, grim, went up the cellar stairs to find a phone. The black one shook his head.

In the living room, Regina abandoned Roger so she could show the young cop to the phone.

When the black officer came up with Thomassy, he said to Ackers, "I'm sorry. I know this is a bad time for you, but I have to ask you to empty your pockets."

"What for?" Ackers shot a look at Thomassy.

"You got a money clip in your pocket?"

Slowly, Ackers withdrew the clip.

"That money yours?" the black cop asked.

"My boy's."

"Can I see that?"

Reluctantly, Ackers handed him the clip. The black officer pulled the bills from it, counted six hundreds, a twenty, and a ten.

"You give him that money?"

Ackers said nothing.

"Where he worked?" the black cop asked. "He must have had one helluva good job."

"Now listen!" Ackers said.

Thomassy said very quietly to the black officer, "You'd probably better let him have his Miranda."

"Yeah. Thanks." The black policeman warned Mr. Ackers of his rights in the conventional terminology, then said, "You gonna tell us where your son worked?"

It was Donald who blurted out from across the room, "He didn't have a job."

Jeb looked like he could have strangled Donald.

"Where'd he get that money then?" asked the cop of Ackers.

"I don't have to say nuthin."

"Empty your pockets," he said.

"What for?"

"Cause we're taking you in."

"You crazy, man?" said Ackers. "He killed my boy and you taking *me* in?"

"Empty your pockets!"

Roger watched Ackers checking his fury. From his left-hand pocket, he took a pack of matches, pulled the pocket out to show it empty, then pushed it back in. From his back pocket, he took out the Afro comb. "You want this?"

"Put it back," said the black cop, his eyes on Ackers's right-hand pocket. "That one," he said.

Ackers withdrew a wrinkled handkerchief. Then a key ring with four keys. The cop kept watching. Ackers took out the switchblade.

The cop held out his hand for the illegal knife. "I'm taking you in," he said.

"I didn't do nuthin, you know I didn't do nuthin!"

"Outside," said the cop, taking Ackers by the arm.

Ackers flung the hand away.

"You shouldna done that, man," said the black cop. He took the handcuffs off his belt.

"You nuts? That mother killed my boy!"

Just then Regina came back from the kitchen, followed by the young cop. As if by signal, the young one grabbed Ackers's arms as the black cop snapped the cuffs on.

"You give me back my boy's money."

"You'll get a receipt at the station house," said the black cop. "Move!"

Roger watched the expression on the young cop's face as, his hand on Ackers's arm, he tugged him toward the door. *He'd kill him in an instant, given the chance.*

Thomassy took advantage of the distraction to get close to Maxwell and whisper, "Get rid of that gun. Give it to me."

"Stuffed it behind the couch pillow," said Roger.

Thomassy nodded.

The children were seeing everything. "You children want to go up and play in the Bestiary?" Regina asked.

When Jeb shook his head, the others shook their heads.

"Okay now," said the black policeman, motioning Roger to follow him.

Roger stepped into the out-of-doors, glad to be out of the Simeon King house. The air smelled cool and clean. Overhead he saw the green hemlock branches stretched in slight curves toward the brightening sky, which now had only occasional wisps of cloud.

The scuffle happened suddenly. Just as the young cop was opening the back door of his car, Ackers swung his cuffed hands hard at the young cop's head, throwing him off balance, then bolted, running, stumbling, toward the thick woods behind the back yard. *He's got a record,* thought Roger, *he's trying to escape.*

While the surprised young cop was getting to his feet, the black officer was already running after Ackers, yelling, "Stop, you in enough trouble," gaining on him, and then, like the athlete he must once have been, he tackled the handcuffed man waist high, bringing him to the ground. The black cop turned to see the young cop standing over Ackers, his pistol drawn.

"Put that away!" he said.

The young cop, livid with embarrassment, holstered his revolver.

"Now see if you can get him into the car."

The youngster hoisted Ackers up, prodded him forward with his hand. All the damn kids were around the front of the house watching.

"I don't have a cage in my car," said the young cop.

"Put him in mine," said the black cop, dusting himself off. "I'll drive him in."

When the black cop drove off with Ackers, the young cop motioned Roger into the other car.

The neighbors will see, thought Roger. *The station is right in the center of town. Everybody will see me getting out.*

Thomassy sensed trouble, came up to Roger fast. "It's just a short ride. I'll follow in my car."

"No," said Roger, and he started walking down the driveway to Fox Lane, his heart beating.

"Where do you think you're going?" yelled the young cop.

Roger had gone perhaps twenty steps, thinking *once people see me in that car, it's all over.*

Thomassy raced after Roger. *I can't let him panic now.* He grabbed Roger by the arm, turned him around, saw the expression on the disgraced cop's face.

Then that crazy kid Jeb was yelling, "My father's got a gun."

"That's not true!" said Thomassy, seeing the young cop pull his gun again.

Regina shook loose from the children, ran past Thomassy, threw her arms around Roger, screening him.

Thomassy ran toward the policeman's young wild eyes, saying, "Don't use unnecessary force."

"You're interfering with an arrest!" the young cop shouted, waving Thomassy away with his gun arm.

God help me, thought Thomassy, *I've got two virgins on my hands.*

As Thomassy strode deliberately toward the policeman, saying, "Let me deal with this," Jeb ran to his mother, and, pulling her by the arm with all his strength, tried dragging her away from Roger, who, as if in a trance, held on to her, his shield, until he could no longer, and the stronger boy pulled her to himself, yelling, "The gun's in his right-hand pocket!"

Thomassy whirled, turning his back to the policeman's gun in time to see Roger's right hand going for his pocket. *That stupid virgin's going to prove his pocket's empty.* "Please, no, don't!" he yelled at Roger, then turned to see the young cop bracing his gun hand on his left arm, and Thomassy shouted, "He's harmless!" but at the last second, as all lawyers must, stepped aside as Regina screamed and the young policeman fired.